A Gen

A Gentlemen's Club

RICHARD GORDON

ARROW BOOKS

To
My Fellow Clubmen

Arrow Books Limited
62-65 Chandos Place, Covent Garden, London WC2N 4NW

An imprint of Century Hutchinson Limited

London Melbourne Sydney Auckland Johannesburg
and agencies throughout the world

First published in Great Britain by Frederick Muller 1988

Arrow edition 1988

Photoset in Palatino by Deltatype Ltd, Ellesmere Port
Printed and bound in Great Britain by
Anchor Brendon Limited, Tiptree, Essex

ISBN 0 09 965360 5

ONE

'Gentlemen are so odd about their clubs.'
Evelyn Waugh, *A Handful of Dust*

1

The stately clubs of London, how complacently they stand!

Boodle's and Brooks's, White's and Pratt's, the Athenaeum and the Travellers', Oxford United with Cambridge, the Carlton and the Reform, the Turf and the Chauffeurs' Arms (as us clubmen call the RAC).

All jammed with haughty anonymity into the square quarter-mile between the Ritz and Eros, the Queen and the ducks in St James's Park.

London has clubs for Alpinists, Flyfishers and Farmers. For Scotsmen and Cavalrymen. For Americans and for Anglo-Belgians. For Liverymen and East Indiamen. For Authors and Eccentrics.

It has the In and Out (as us clubmen call the Naval and Military). The Arts Club. The Railway Club. The National Liberal and the Kennel.

Fifty gentlemen's clubs!

Where well-tailored gentlemen disappear through stout doors guarded by liveried porters, exclusively to enjoy each other's company in an atmosphere reputedly reeking so desirably of port and pheasant.

Everyone in the country who aims to be anyone makes use of gentlemen's clubs, like the public schools and Moss Bros.

Gossip columnists are fascinated by them. The populace is bemused by them. People speculate about the goings-on inside as nosily as inside Number Ten or Wormwood Scrubs.

Come with me.

Let me escort you from Pall Mall, up steps worn by five

generations of gentlemanly leather, into the Albany Club.

I am the Oldest Member.

An enviable status, which prolongs 'the happiest days of your life' to the grave. Though this is perhaps an irrelevance, because none of the older members can remember who is dead or who is not.

Come with me on that memorable summer morning when our steps were timorously mounted by a *beautiful young lady*.

'Madam?'

Hawkins, our claret-liveried porter, glared from his glass cubicle inside the front door.

'Can I help you?' he enquired, freezingly unhelpful.

The visitor gave a nervous smile.

The Albany Club has been sensitive to ladies' liberation since the Suffragettes smashed our windows in 1908.

After Hitler had repeated the violation – I was obliged to take shelter all night in the wine-cellar – a Queen returned to the throne. The Albany was founded under Victoria, when the middle classes flooded London with gentlemen eager to meet other gentlemen to convince themselves that they were.

We then began to take ladies' aspirations seriously.

Dinner became heterosexual.

Naturally, segregated in a brand-new ladies' dining room, with a club ladies' entrance submissive to the erect columns of the gentlemen's portico.

This lady explained shyly to Hawkins: 'I'm Miss Ann Frobisher. The new assistant club secretary.'

'Indeed, madam!'

Hawkins gazed in horror towards the vaulted roof of the entrance hall, relieved to hear: 'Good morning. I'm the secretary. Wing Commander Browne.'

The Gallant Winco! A squat gentleman in his summer uniform of double-breasted brass-buttoned blue blazer and striped RAF tie, advancing with formally welcoming hand down our chessboard-floored hall bulwarked with hat-racks.

The Albany Club knew that to survive it needed to express that British genius for lurching with the times, which has so splendidly saved similar crusted institutions as Wimbledon, Harrods and the Royal Family.

We had long employed 'nippies', despite members' grumbles about needing to watch their language over lunch. When the Queen appointed a lady prime minister, we conceded that the Albany might safely appoint a lady cashier.

Only a gentleman whom the Sovereign trusted with a commission was hitherto thought trustworthy with the Albany Club secrets.

The creation of Miss Frobisher as his assistant – and more awesomely, eventual successor – nearly brought an epidemic of the heart attacks to which our members are so distressingly liable.

'Sorry hadn't met when the committee appointed you,' the Gallant Winco apologized gruffly. 'Been on leave.'

'I can't tell you how overwhelmed I am, working in a gentlemen's club,' ventured Miss Frobisher, dark and green-eyed, smoothly moulding a Liberty lawn blouse.

The Gallant Winco was puzzled. 'Oh? Really?'

'I hope I shall measure up to the gentlemen.'

'Public have quite the wrong impression of gentlemen's clubs,' the Gallant Winco reassured her kindly. 'They think we're privileged, reactionary, chauvinistic. Ridiculous!' he scoffed.

'What is a club but the sum of its members?' he demanded philosophically. 'Here at the Albany, they're all courteous, intelligent, worldly men, who've made some success of their lives. Otherwise they'd never be elected. What? This is the morning room.'

The morning room beyond the hall admittedly reflects the popular image of gentlemen's clubs – gloomy chambers with plush curtains and sombre pictures, littered with leather armchairs in which gentlemen read *The Times*, decide *Punch* not as good as it was, drink port and snore.

'Where the members sit in the morning?' suggested Miss Frobisher brightly.

'No, no! The members aren't here in the morning.'

'And that's the dining room,' she redeemed herself.

'The coffee room,' the Gallant Winco corrected her.

'Where the members take coffee.'

'No, no! That's where they eat. They take coffee in the morning room.'

'Wing Commander,' she confessed disarmingly. 'I see I've a lot to learn.'

The Gallant Winco looked round furtively.

'No one about. This is the members' bog.'

He pushed open a plain oak door beside the life-sized statue of Mr Gladstone.

'But how magnificent!' exclaimed Miss Frobisher wonderingly, inspecting our gleaming row of urinals. 'It's like the Elgin Marbles, put to good use.'

'What?' The Gallant Winco was lost.

'That mahogony seating!' she admired. 'Those lovely brass handles! Those chains – they could raise Tower Bridge. And who might they be?' she asked, eyeing curiously the framed drawings of gentlemen on the tiled walls.

'Deceased members. The committee selects them.'

The Gallant Winco coughed. There was something of which he needed to relieve his mind. This seemed the place to do it.

'Miss Frobisher. May I make it absolutely plain that I was not in the slightest upset, hurt, concerned or surprised when the committee made you my assistant.'

'Wing Commander, may I make it absolutely plain that I was utterly astonished.'

'Oh? Why?'

'After a life in the Air Force, I thought you wouldn't at all care to work with a woman.'

'Ah! But that's the thing about the Services,' he considerately corrected her. 'Teaches you to work with absolutely anyone. Chinks, coolies, crackpots, crooks. Don't imagine I've anything against women. They've the same size brain as men, so they tell me.'

Then Herbert arrived.

Outside the bog hangs a portrait of William Makepeace Thackeray – a member of the Albany – with his pebble glasses and his condescending bulk. In the days when soldiers wore Waterloo medals, his Major Pendennis arrived with the best-blacked boots in London at his Pall Mall club at ten-fifteen every morning for his breakfast.

Today, Herbert similarly quits his bus in Haymarket and strolls to the Albany every weekday of his life.

He is a gentleman as respected inside the Albany Club as outside it he is unnoticed, or I sometimes suspect even exists.

He bid 'Good morning' to Hawkins. He had long since abandoned asking for letters, Herbert not being the sort that anyone had interest in writing to and less in hearing from.

He hung his brown trilby on his customary brass peg and paused. A young lady was emerging from the bog.

She seemed a pretty young lady, but he had not his glasses on.

'There's a member here in the morning,' whispered Miss Frobisher, noticing Herbert's spare, tall figure.

'That's Mr Smallove,' the Gallant Winco explained helpfully. 'He's always here.'

'Always?' Her eyes widened.

'Yes. Arrives when the club opens. Leaves at night when it shuts.'

'You mean, every day?'

He was incredulous at her incredulity.

'Except in August, when we're closed to be cleaned. Then he can go next door to the Cavendish.'

'Hasn't he a home?' Miss Frobisher enquired tenderly.

'Home? Well. Don't know. Not the sort of thing you'd ask.'

'How pathetic!' she breathed.

'Pathetic?' asked the Gallant Winco huffily. 'Why?'

'I mean, the poor man having to spend all his life in his club.'

The Gallant Winco was baffled. 'What's wrong with that? This is a place a lot of gentlemen would give their eye teeth to get into.'

Herbert passed with a silent nod into the morning room, selected *The Times* from a table festooned with the daily and weekly press, and took his favourite chair between the bust of Lord Curzon and the padded brass and leather bum-warmer round the hearth, where every day he contributed little more to the Club conversation than the brightly polished fire irons.

2

Only Herbert sat in the morning room in the mornings.

Two hours later, gentlemen started shoaling into the calm Albany backwater from the buffeting London currents, in time for one before lunch – or two, or three, or possibly a skinful.

George and Aubrey arrived simultaneously.

'Guess what day it is?' George invited Hawkins breezily.

'Wednesday, sir. Steak and kidney pie day.'

'Publication day!' George corrected him.

George is a novelist, like Thackeray.

Aubrey exclaimed admiringly: 'Congratulations! Must be frightfully exciting, being an author, old boy.'

'When my first book came out,' George recalled wistfully, 'I leapt out of bed, threw open the window and expected the world to be different. I was so charmingly young, so attractively naïve! I could as well have expected Father Christmas to appear down the chimney. Here's a yeasty new loaf, cast upon the world's oceans of indifference.'

He flourished at Hawkins the shiny jacketed *Age Cannot Wither*, A Novel, by George Gifford. From the back stared a photograph before his wavy-haired, sharp romantic looks had suffered erosion by the pleasurable pollution of life.

'Another one for the club library,' George directed.

'Very good, sir.'

'They all get pinched, anyway,' George told Aubrey resignedly.

George wrote 'significant' novels, very much for our time – you know the sort of thing. The critics loved him. It was sadly not a promiscuous affair. Few bought George's books. Even Albany members could no longer be bothered to steal them.

Such is the literary world of which the Albany is a flourishing outpost.

George has grown disillusioned, and can become as sour as the club 'economy' champagne.

He sometimes declares shockingly that the only literary superiority of a book over television is the necessity of knowing how to read, which is not exacting.

The poor fellow does not make much out of it.

He had a tarty young wife, but she bolted.

'What are you doing this afternoon?' he asked Aubrey, as they entered the hall.

'Earning a crust in the City.'

Aubrey suffered the distressing waggishness infesting gentlemen's clubs.

'Pity. You could have come to see the author signing copies in a Piccadilly bookshop. Ghastly business! People circle round staring and grinning, as though you were a one-man band performing on a street corner. They never seem to buy anything. But people don't much in bookshops.'

'Then why suffer, dear boy?'

'Books come on sale and return, you know,' George revealed. 'Sign everything in sight, then they're spoiled copies. The bookseller can't get his money back, he's got to sell 'em, probably to his relatives. And I get my royalty. Writers stop the idealistic dreamer bit when it comes to cash, you know.'

Aubrey seemed shocked – in a mild, gentlemanly way – at such application of City attitudes to culture.

'Why, I think I've signed quite a lot of other authors' books in my time, by mistake,' George confessed cheerfully.

He stopped. He anxiously fingered his satin bow tie. Then confronted Miss Frobisher.

'May I direct you to the ladies' entrance?' Aubrey always displayed gentlemanly quick-wittedness on the scene of nasty social accidents.

Half-smiling, faintly blushing, she imparted modestly: 'I'm afraid I'm the new assistant secretary.'

Both agreed this was delightful.

'Haven't been matron of a boys' school, I suppose?' Aubrey suggested, worseningly waggish. 'That would help enormously.'

'Only training in hotel management, sir. In France.'

George announced sweepingly: 'Then I'm sure we'll see an improvement in the food, which is uneatable, and in the wine, which is undrinkable. The Winco, however gallant, never even learned to run a vindaloo takeaway.'

'What were you doing before that?' asked Aubrey politely.

'I was a vicar's daughter, sir.'

'Now, no mucking about with the menu.' Aubrey became waggish to the forefinger under her *retroussé* nose. 'Can't do without my daily prunes.'

'Gets dreadfully constipated,' George volunteered.

'I would never interfere with the club traditions, sir,' she assured him.

The two members wandered towards the morning room.

Aubrey Whitaker was a florid gentleman, a stockbroker, his riches mitigated by an extravagant wife called Gloria.

Both clubmen were 'good eggs', and close friends.

That George once spent a fortnight in Cannes with Gloria when Aubrey was in New York, I was the only member of the Albany to know.

Including Aubrey.

Miss Frobisher noticed on a small hard chair beneath the chiselled disdain of Lord Palmerston – against the wrought-iron stand from which members plaintively complain on the club notice board that their umbrellas have been taken (always 'by mistake') – one who was neither a clubman nor gentleman.

She recalled him sitting there through the emotional turmoil of her entrance.

He rose. 'Excuse me–'.

He was small and bald, with a tight blue suit and a bulging black briefcase.

'Did I overhear you were the assistant secretary?'

He had that voice heard raising awkward questions from the back at public meetings.

'Yes – but it's my first day.'

'I've been waiting to see the secretary. For two hours and forty-two minutes.'

'Oh, I'm so sorry!' Miss Frobisher apologized earnestly. 'Was it a matter of importance?'

'No longer. I have simply closed the kitchen.'

She was puzzled.

He drew breath.

'Three months ago, I performed my duty as environmental health officer by inspecting your kitchen. What did I find? Grease. Dirt. Droppings. Cockroaches. Mice and rats, alive and dead. Feral cats, I seem to remember. Birds nesting above the fish steamer. The toilets separated from the handwashing facilities by the cold meats and salads. When I complained the staff were smoking, they rudely asked how they were expected to put up with the smell.'

Miss Frobisher gave a fluttering gasp.

'May I say, the kitchen of the Albany Club would have disgraced a Victorian East End dosshouse.'

The inspector paused, mouth a rod of iron.

'I sought an interview – several interviews – with the secretary. He seemed to think that kitchens were beneath the dignity of his nose to stick into. I had no alternative but to ban your kitchen from providing food for human beings, an activity for which it is as unsuited as the Barking Creek sewer.'

She exclaimed: 'But we have to serve lunch in an hour's time!'

'I advise you to send out for some sandwiches. Good morning.'

'Surely there's something we can put right?' She offered desperately: 'I'll get on my hands and knees with a scrubbing-brush, if you like.'

'Put right? I will not reopen those kitchens until they undergo total modernization.'

'But the poor members won't get their daily nourishing lunch,' she told him in anguish.

'There's nothing that £10,000 won't cure.'

'But we haven't got £10,000!' she imparted.

He smirked. 'What, a gentlemen's club? Haunt of the rich and privileged.'

'Some of our gentlemen are very poor. Honestly! They've nowhere else to pass the day. This is their home.'

'I recommend the British Museum. It's got a clean cafeteria. Good morning,' he repeated, opening the front door.

She grabbed him. 'Please! Wait a minute. Would you like a cup of coffee?'

'Coffee! I wouldn't risk anything out of that place.'

'Just hold on. Please . . . please . . .'

A man with a mouth – or even soul – of iron could not resist Miss Frobisher's glance. She looked as imploring as Desdemona with Othello reaching for the pillow.

In the morning room, the Gallant Winco was into his first of the day.

He had joined George and Aubrey in a 'pinkers'.

Pink gin! Angostura bitters, like pungent drops of blood, mixed with a large Plymouth gin and cooled Malvern water, the horsepower of the Royal Navy from the Falklands of 1914 to the Falklands of 1982, the communion-wine of the clubman classes.

'I think it best,' he said awkwardly, as Miss Frobisher appeared breathlessly, 'if you don't come in the members' rooms before lunchtime. Gives 'em a bit of a turn, seeing a lady.'

'That's the point, Wing Commander. There isn't going to be any lunchtime.'

'What?'

'A man from the council has just shut the kitchen.'

'What!'

'I've just been down there. The staff are all going home.'

'But they can't!' he cried in disbelief. 'It's steak and kidney pie day. The members all look forward to it.'

'You really must see this inspector, Wing Commander.' She had the fondly firm air of mother with a difficult child. 'He seems a leftover from *Oliver Twist*.'

The Gallant Winco grunted, obligingly gulped his pinkers and disobligingly left.

'What *is* going on, Brindles?' Aubrey asked the wine steward.

'Some nosey parker's been in the kitchen half the morning, sir. Lifting up the toilet seats and poking his fingers in the soup.'

'How disgusting.'

'He did carry on, sir, about my cats. Poor little creatures!' said the kindly man.

Brindles was small, bent, wispy-haired, in shining white jacket, crisp napkin over arm, gleaming silver tray in hand. He had been serving drinks in the morning room longer than I can remember, and I can remember when a pinkers cost ninepence.

'The pussies come in from the cold, sir, it's nice for them round the stove. I give them a little nibble of the members' fish, and the milk when it's going off.'

'I suppose we're a "catering establishment",' George suggested fairly. 'Like any other geriatric home of rest.'

'Oh, the Gallant Winco will shoot him down,' declared Aubrey confidently.

They fell silent a while. So smooth is the surface of club life, any unexpected ruffle is as disquieting as the occult gyrations of the Loch Ness monster.

3

Club conversation resumed.

Michael Arlen's art déco heroine Iris Storm complained in *The Green Hat* that distinguished Englishmen pass their lives *bantering*.

Arlen was a foreigner – an Armenian, you cannot get more foreign than that – but became a naturalized clubman. He was a member of the Garrick, which is rather theatrical, and the Savage, which is rather savage.

Herbert meanwhile read *The Times*, stared at Rudyard Kipling on the wall or drummed his fingertips together, ignored as usual by the chatterers like a favourite dog on the hearthrug.

'Is this were I go?'

A handsome young man in a stylish suit had wandered from the hall. He announced mildly: 'I'm a new member.'

Aubrey automatically offered him a drink.

'How kind. I'll have a *crème de menthe frappée*. And not great blocks of ice.'

'Very good, sir.' Brindles acquiesced respectfully.

Queer choice, Aubrey thought. Pinkers and champers were the tolerated tipple, not pansy ones ordered in French.

'Fantastic room!' The newcomer's eye swept it like a lighthouse beam.

'Glad you like it,' George congratulated his taste.

He laughed. 'I don't actually *like* it. It's such an exquisite period piece.'

The atmosphere became *frappée*.

'*We* rather like it,' Aubrey told him.

'Oh, I'm sure I shall. When I get used to it.'

George's voice bristled. 'The pictures have been much admired.'

The new boy looked incredulous.

'That one has been ascribed to Turner,' Aubrey enlightened him.

'It's a fake, isn't it?' he mentioned casually, inspecting the golden glow against sepia mountains and ochre cattle, which I have secretly believed an ancient whisky advertisement.

'What's your line of country?' asked George inquisitively.

'I'm an interior decorator.'

He took *The Times* from Herbert's lap, sat down and started on the crossword.

Brindles presented the drink.

He reached in his pocket and placed one pound on the silver tray.

'Oh, sir!' cried Brindles in horror.

The young man looked surprised. 'It's for you.'

'That would *never* do, sir! Gratuities are absolutely forbidden in the club, sir. Like talking business, sir. Oh dear, sir!'

'What a funny old thing!' The new member pocketed

the coin, Brindles withdrawing with expression by H M Bateman.

'He's a beloved old club servant,' George told him severely.

The gentlemanly servants – each a Weller, Figaro, Sancho, Jeeves – consummate a gentlemen's club. They know each member's desires and idiosyncrasies, which they dutifully tend unbidden, uncomplaining and unamazed.

Members reared in the delicate, intimate relationship between master and fag, gyp, scout, bedder, batman, ghillie, *au pair* girl, are equally proud of their sensitive touch with the staff, which they apply outside to bus conductors, head waiters, meter attendants, policemen, and other menials.

'I expect his lovable qualities will grow on me. Aren't you George Gifford, the writer? I saw you on the telly last night.'

George looked pleased.

'Plugging your latest novel.'

George looked less pleased.

'What else should I know about this place?'

'These days, you can bring your wife to lunch,' Aubrey told him.

'Oh, I'm not *married*.'

'There's the library upstairs. It contains an original Dickens' manuscript.'

'We'd be grateful for your telling us if that's a fake, too,' George invited.

'Delighted.'

He tossed aside *The Times* and ascended the sweeping staircase, where Disraeli slid down the banisters after winning the election of 1874.

'What *are* the committee admitting?' asked George wearily, once the new gentleman was beyond earshot.

'He's a queer,' declared Aubrey firmly. 'A screaming poofter. I mean! Interior decorator and *crème de menthe*.'

'What of it?' demanded George fair-mindedly. 'Oscar Wilde's as dead as Queen Anne, darling.'

'Oh, I know we must keep up with the times,' Aubrey agreed resignedly. 'Otherwise, we become a ridiculous curiosity, like a herd of dinosaurs browsing in St James's Park. But I don't like the idea. Not a bit. Look at that girl they've appointed as assistant secretary.'

'Women now are acceptable in all branches of society.' George finished his pinkers. 'Like poofters. I think she's delicious.'

'That's not the point. If I want delicious women, I can go elsewhere.'

'Do tell?' George invited.

'Dr Johnson defined a club as an assembly of good fellows, meeting under certain conditions. I don't regard screaming poofters as good fellows,' Aubrey ended disgruntledly.

He was interrupted by a cheerful crowd of gentlemen arriving from the hall, with neat suits, firmly knotted ties, speckless collars and shoes.

A club at any day is formed by its members who casually decide to drop in for lunch. It changes as unexpectedly as the London sky – dull, lively, humorous, learned, contentious or drunken.

'Steak and kidney pie day!' Rollo sniffed cheerfully. 'You can always tell what's for lunch, wafting up the back stairs. God knows why they bother to type menus.'

'Someone's been at *The Times* crossword,' exclaimed Bertie angrily. 'How dare they! I always like to do it myself.'

They all ordered pinkers and champers.

'God, here's Willi,' Rollo groaned, staring through the open morning-room door down the hall.

'He's being very generous towards the club,' Aubrey defended him, in a gentlemanly way.

'Only because he's as desperate to get on the committee as into the House of Lords.'

'Willi always reminds me of a line by Ogden Nash,'

George meditated. 'You know, the American poet. "To be an Englishman is to belong to the most exclusive club there is".'

'Willi really is a prize stinker,' Bertie muttered, adding with hearty friendliness: 'Hello Willi!'

'Hello, boys! Brindles, my favourite tipple.'

Willi came from Posnan, or Pilsen, or Potsdam or some other faraway country with people of whom clubmen were only too pleased to know nothing, as Neville Chamberlain said about the Czechs, or possibly the Poles. Applying an ungentlemanly shrewdness and industry to his enterprises, he now had a finger in many juicy, fruity pies.

Becoming a millionaire, he did not, like the Englishmen he had joined, retire to an Old Rectory or Home Farm and dissipate his remaining years harmlessly with husbandry and good works. He became a multi-millionaire, widely considered in the Albany Club as overdoing things a bit.

'Look at these letters!' Willi brandished a handful of envelopes at the morning room. 'I tell people never write to me here, or I shall be thought a naughty boy doing business in the club, eh?'

Willi was huge, dark-haired and dark-jowled, his accent wearing English expressions as awkwardly as a Chinaman a bowler. Any restaurant where he was unable to behave entirely as he pleased he could instantly leave, or purchase. But he revelled in the discipline of a club. Because, like a virtuous woman, its price was far above rubies.

'George, you were on my television channel last night,' he continued jovially. 'I have sent my secretary out to buy several copies of your latest book. Aubrey, did I see in *The Times* you're organizing a charity for the handicapped children of City workers? Put me down for a grand, eh? Don't forget.'

He took a silver tankard of champagne from Brindles'

tray. 'The dear old club! What a haven of rest! Cheers, chaps! Ah, lunch!'

Brindles had struck a note on the gong, as if starting one of Lord Rank's old movies.

'I am quite as hungry as a hunter.' Willi departed with relish to the dining room, which we call the coffee room. 'Steak and kidney pie day! What bliss, eh?'

'I have just had the unsettling experience of meeting a new member who is vain, brash, vulgar and homosexual,' Aubrey declared despondently to the others.

'At least he wasn't . . . er,' commented Rollo cheerfully.

'I suppose it's extremely immoral, if not illegal, of us to have no members who are . . . er,' George reflected.

'I once had a lovely girlfriend who was absolutely . . . er, all over,' chuckled Bertie.

'However desperate we are to keep up with the times, I can guarantee that anybody who was . . . er, would never get elected to the Albany,' said Aubrey firmly. 'And I'm being neither immoral nor illegal. I'm simply stating a fact.'

An Englishman's club is his castle, and two black balls exclude.

4

The kitchen of the Albany Club resembled the kitchens of Cruikshank, 'Phiz' and Leech – coaching-inn kitchens, workhouse kitchens, thieves' kitchens, their drawings of Dickens' images endure like tombstones. (Dickens regrettably was not a member, he was terrified that Thackeray would blackball him.)

'Grease.'

The inspector ran his finger inside the club fridge, regarding the sticky blob on the end with the gratification of a gourmet about to consume some delicious *bonne bouche*.

'Rancid, with it. Been there for years, I'd say. Left over from Christmas?' He produced a tooth-marked drumstick. 'Not last Christmas.'

'Look here, I'm not going to be told how to run my kitchen by someone from the corporation drains department,' the Gallant Winco corrected the social situation.

The inspector drew a stiff mouse from the dry-store cupboard by its tail. 'If you must have the place full of cats, you might see they do their job.'

'Permit me, inspector.' Miss Frobisher smilingly relieved him of the corpse, which she coffined in a silver entrée dish.

'This club, I'll have you know, has many distinguished members who give great service to the country,' the Gallant Winco countered the insanitary insinuations.

'All the more reason they should not meet an untimely death from botulism.'

'Impossible! The club contains many eminent doctors.'

The inspector looked round dreamily. 'When I take some specimens from this kitchen, our laboratory will have a field day. A regular field day.'

The three stood by the dumb waiter, watched by a pair of white-hatted young chefs and an aproned old man leaning on a mop smoking his pipe. A shrill whistle sounded from the coffee room above.

'Twelve steak and kidney four with mash eight with chips,' screamed our pretty Cockney 'nippy' Rosie down the lift shaft.

The inspector's eye glinted. 'I utterly forbid any article of food whatsoever leaving this disgusting kitchen.'

The Gallant Winco's eye had an enemy aircraft in its gunsight. 'And I utterly forbid anyone whatsoever keeping my members from their lunch.'

He pressed the button.

The load of tin-capped plates shot upwards.

The inspector pressed the button.

They came down again.

'Ere!' screeched Rosie. 'What you bleeding well doing with my steak and kidneys?'

The Gallant Winco fired once more.

Then he protected the button with his own blazered body.

He grinned, as though the enemy aircraft had exploded in flames and the pilot's parachute failed to open.

'My members will be getting hungry.'

'I am giving the orders here,' snapped the militant civilian.

'Don't be so damn cheeky.'

'Do you realize that I can telephone Cannon Row police station? For a policeman to arrest you, for obstructing me in the course of my duty?'

'Can't arrest me. I'm a Wing Commander.'

Rosie blew the whistle. 'What you lot up to, down there? Gone bleeding bonkers?'

'I've had enough! I'm getting the police.'

'Won't do the slightest good. The club contains many learned judges.'

Rosie blew the whistle again.

'*Please* inspector–'

Miss Frobisher had observed the clash of cultures with amazement, confusion, horror.

'You have to make allowances for the Wing Commander,' she explained sweetly. 'He's suffered these attacks since his unpleasant experience with a German over Beachy Head.'

'What? What?' demanded the Gallant Winco.

'I'm sorry he's a war casualty. There's still going to be no lunch,' the inspector responded unsympathetically.

The whistle blew.

'For God's sake go up and stop that woman behaving like a football referee,' the Gallant Winco instructed testily.

We later discovered that Miss Frobisher combined the assiduity of Florence Nightingale with the management skills of Mrs Beeton, the *élan* of Joan of Arc and the determination of Lady Macbeth.

Her only concern, her first day, was if it were always like this.

'Gentlemen!'

She struck a note on the gong at the door of the coffee room.

'I have two announcements to make. First, I am your new assistant secretary.'

From the long, polished table with its beautiful silver and linen napkins, set against portraits of fierce generals and gloomy bishops, came shouts across the cut-glass decanters of club claret: 'Jolly good!' 'Shame!' 'Splendid!' mixed with clapping and wolf whistles.

'Secondly, there will be no lunch today. Good morning.'

Hungry, but well-bred noises, like the pack of the Quorn in full cry.

'I'm sorry. But a man from the health department has shut the kitchen as insanitary.'

Fierce snorts, like the pack of the Quorn scenting blood.

Rollo looked indignant. 'Isn't the Gallant Winco coping?'

'Yes. But he needs £10,000.'

'We'll have a whip-round,' suggested Aubrey at once.

Silence.

'Won't we?' he asked pathetically.

'Boys–'

Willi rose at the head of the table.

'I offer the club a loan of £10,000. Absolutely interest free. To be repaid whenever the club feels like it. How's that?'

Silence.

'Interest free . . .' he repeated pathetically.

Aubrey hissed to George: 'I find particularly revolting the way he rubs the club's nose into his money.'

Willi was a gentleman of action.

'I will see this fellow myself. Take me to him, please,' he requested Miss Frobisher. 'I'm sure we can sort it out in a shake of braces.'

The members looked at each other in dismay. There was nothing to do but finish the claret.

5

I had evaded the grip of starvation on the club.

I had walked to Pall Mall on that shimmering summer morning, when even the red buses amid the choking London traffic wore a vulgar cheerfulness.

Arriving late, and needing to verify a quotation from Gibbon, I ascended the spiral stone staircase beyond the porter's box to the library on the top floor, which I entered through a narrow door amusingly camouflaged inside as shelves of books, startling a handsome young man in a stylish suit flicking through bound volumes of the *Illustrated London News*.

I introduced myself.

He responded: 'Harker-Hewitt. A new member.'

'I'm a very old one, I suppose. You'll find up here a useful spot for peace and quiet. The members aren't very bookish. You'll soon get the hang of the place. Only the unwritten rules matter.'

'Not doing business in the club?'

'Dear boy, more business is done in London clubs than in Throgmorton Street and Petticoat Lane put together.'

I scanned the shelf for *Decline and Fall of the Roman Empire*.

'No, always being polite, sweet-tempered, good-humoured, and ready with cheerful conversation,' I instructed him. 'In the face of behaviour which is generally eccentric, often aggravating and sometimes infuriating. It can be a strain.'

Drawing out the volume, I continued: 'You know, if people applied to marital relations the care applied to club ones, divorce would become as obsolete as the ducking-stool. Ah! here we are: "Twenty-two acknowledged concubines, and a library of sixty-two thousand volumes, attested the variety of his inclinations, and from the productions which he left behind him, it appears that the former as well as the latter were designed for use rather than ostentation." That was Gordianus the Second. Such realistic, catholic, intelligent and constructive hedonism marks him a typical clubman.'

I snapped the book shut.

'I've only met three members. One was George Gifford–'

'Then the others would be Aubrey Whitaker and Herbert Smallove, who says nothing. A club is the sum of its cliques. Anonymity is another unwritten rule,' I mentioned helpfully. 'We had an American diplomat here, enjoying a year's exchange from the Century Club in New York, who sat at the long table for lunch, immediately told his neighbours his name and actually *shook hands* with them. The horror created had him sitting silent upon his hands whenever taking his seat thereafter. He wrote later that he had met many amusing, erudite and charming people at the Albany Club. He only wished he knew who they were.'

I replaced the Gibbon. Did our unwritten rules condemn George for becoming a shareholder in Aubrey's wife? Had it got round the members, would

George have suffered the appalling fate of Wilde's Lord Kelso, who 'ate his chop alone at the club for some time afterwards'?

I fancied not. Unless of course George had done it on the club premises.

'You mentioned a ducking-stool. What's that?'

'A gout-stool.'

Harker-Hewitt indicated beside Plato's bust a two-foot mahogany board thickly upholstered with tasselled satin, a single foot at one end.

'A distressingly common complaint among the port-drinking classes. You tucked the free end between thigh and chair, raising the gouty toe to the easeful horizontal. The doctors have some infallible cure now, I believe, but the Albany is a conservative and sceptical society which prefers to retain them poised for instant action. I'm keeping you from your lunch.'

He glanced at the solemn-ticking Victorian wall clock.

'No, I've a rather late lunch date in Soho, with a girl in the rag trade. I suppose the club's got a loo?'

'Between the morning room and the hall, just past Mr Gladstone.'

I strolled with him towards the main staircase.

'The club food's awful,' I warned. 'You know Shaw's remark: "An Englishman thinks he is moral when he is only uncomfortable"? It's another of our English perversions – the suspicion of good food in any institution not exclusively for that purpose. I remember, my Cambridge college took pride that the food was terrible. We were up there for the learning, not the cooking. I used to bring a hard-boiled egg and a bottle of beer in my briefcase to eat up here,' I revealed. 'But the wretched secretary made a frightful fuss over charging me cappage.'

6

Enjoying also the resourcefulness of Grace Darling, Miss Frobisher grabbed a bottle of Albany Club brandy as she passed the kitchen's pudding corner with bustling Willi.

The inspector and the Gallant Winco were still beside the dumb waiter, glowering.

'Can I offer you a little something?'

Miss Frobisher handed the inspector a coffee cup of brandy.

'We're all getting a weeny bit over-excited, aren't we?'

She was mother, when the birthday beano ended in tears.

'Why don't you take a seat, inspector?' she asked kindly, sweeping a pair of cats off a kitchen chair.

'I'm sure the Wing Commander realizes that you're only doing your duty – as he once did his so gallantly.'

'What? What?' murmured the Gallant Winco absently, filling a teacup with brandy.

'My dear chappie!'

Willi had been staring round appraisingly.

'I expect you have inspected the kitchens of the Princess Elizabeth Hotel in Park Lane?' he suggested politely.

All four looked upwards. Loud gurgles resounded from the curved pipe that led through the ceiling from the members' lavatory.

'I have,' the inspector told him bleakly. He calculated that the continued ferocity of the Gallant Winco's expression justified a sip of brandy.

A satisfied grin enlivened Willi's heavy jowls. 'Then we have something in common.'

'You eat in it?'

'I own it. Perhaps there is room for improvement here–'

Willi swept his arm towards the Dickensian panorama.

'But couldn't you, inspector, turn a blind eye? Like our great Nelson, who had one eye and one leg?'

'One arm,' the Gallant Winco corrected him gruffly.

'Wasn't it one leg?' returned Willi snappily.

'Haven't you seen him, up the bloody pole?'

'Funny thing,' Willi reflected. 'I happen to own a kitchen equipment company. If my chappies started work next Monday morning, they could have the place modernized in a month. Who pays, we can settle afterwards, as among pals, eh?' he directed to the Gallant Winco.

The inspector sipped brandy silently.

'It is so easy to forget little matters of hygiene in a busy kitchen, eh?' Willi invited generously: 'Will you help me out? Come to the Princess Elizabeth one evening, keep us up to the mark. We pay a fee for your trouble, naturally.'

The inspector sipped.

'Stay for dinner,' Willi suggested enthusiastically. 'We have a new chef. From the Tour d'Argent in Paris.' He kissed his fingertips. 'I've a better idea! Come for the weekend. Bring the wife. The kiddiwinks, too. We are bound to have a penthouse suite free.'

The inspector finished his brandy.

'You guarantee this work will be done?'

Willi shot out his hand.

'I give you my word – as an Englishman.'

'I will allow a stay of execution till Monday.'

'Hurrah!' cried the Gallant Winco, giving the victory sign, though magnanimously behind the inspector's back and in reverse.

The inspector sniffed. 'Do I smell drains?'

'Drains?' The Gallant Winco was incredulous. 'No drains within hundreds of yards. Keep 'em all outside.'

He sniffed louder.

'I fancy I know a drain when I smell one.'

'This club brandy really is jolly good,' Willi recommended, refilling the coffee cup.

'Miss Frobisher–' The Gallant Winco grabbed her arm. He hissed: 'It's the members' bog. Overflowing as usual. For God's sake, go up and fix it.'

Miss Frobisher hurried bravely through the oak door beside the statute of Mr Gladstone. The magnificent apartment was vacant.

She saw a mahogany-seated closet flooding the marble floor, grabbed the ever-ready suction pole from its bucket of pungent disinfectant, and plied it like an Edwardian washerwoman at the tub.

Harker-Hewitt entered, unzipping.

'Ann!' he cried. 'Darling!'

Miss Frobisher looked up.

'Quentin! Darling!'

Harker-Hewitt grabbed Miss Frobisher, kissing her fiercely.

'What are you doing here?' he asked incredulously.

'I'm the new assistant secretary,' Miss Frobisher told him breathlessly.

'What, left that lovely hotel in St Tropez?'

Harker-Hewitt laughed. 'What a summer! All that nude bathing.'

Miss Frobisher giggled. 'All those nude barbecues.'

'I must see you again! I must!' Harker-Hewitt insisted.

'No, darling, no,' Miss Frobisher protested desperately, as Harker-Hewitt grasped her to him, fondling her corsage. 'You know it was all over.'

'Yes! You *must* let me.'

'No, you *mustn't*!' Miss Frobisher cried, silenced with a crushing kiss.

George and Aubrey walked in.

George and Aubrey walked out again.

They stood outside the door.

'You know,' decided Aubrey after a moment's reflection. 'I think I owe that chap something of an apology.'

7

Most members had despaired of lunch.

I sat at the head of the table beside Willi, consuming my steak and kidney followed by jam roly-poly and hot custard, while he recounted expansively how he became the saviour of the kitchens.

This took until the coffee and port.

'So, everything downstairs will soon be spick and span and Bristol fashion,' Willi concluded smugly. 'And who pays, who cares? We are all in the same boat, eh?'

Gentlemen had been leaving steadily during the vivid recital, so precipitously it was necessary to gulp their port. We were alone.

Willi spread his big hands on the polished table-top.

'All's well that ends well, eh? Perhaps after that spot of bother,' he suggested solemnly, 'you would consider putting me up for the committee?'

I wiped my mouth with my linen napkin.

'No.'

He looked amazed.

'But why, old chappie? Did you want to go without lunch?'

'May I say, Willi – with the full frankness and friendship of a fellow-clubman – that rather than you pay for our kitchen, I should prefer to starve to death.'

I rose.

I left.

I heard behind me the baffled and miserable exclamation: 'I can never understand us English.'

Herbert was alone in the morning room.

'Brindles,' he instructed, as the bell was answered. 'Will you get me something?'

'Of course, sir.'

'I will have a small glass of port.'

'But sir!' Brindles looked shocked. 'You never have anything to drink in the club, sir.'

There was a pause.

'Today is my seventieth birthday.'

'Oh, sir!' said Brindles.

All that we love in our club was in his voice.

TWO

1

What more cheering in everyday life than always being welcome, even if you hardly go anywhere.

'Good morning, Mr Smallove!' said Hawkins warmly from his glass cubicle. 'Splendid weather. No letters, I'm afraid, as usual.'

With a silent smile, Herbert passed across the chess-board-floored hall to hang his hat. Hawkins's head shook sadly behind him.

'The poor gentleman,' he muttered. 'I don't think he knows anyone to write to.'

'Good morning, sir!' said Brindles assiduously, polishing glasses beside Mr Gladstone. 'Wednesday again, sir. Steak and kidney pie day.'

With a silent smile, Herbert passed into the morning room.

'Good morning, Mr Smallove!' said Miss Frobisher charmingly. 'Lovely day for Ascot, isn't it?'

With a silent smile, Herbert took *The Times* from the newspaper table and settled into his favourite chair under the nose of Lord Curzon.

'Brindles,' confessed Miss Frobisher, sidling up to Mr Gladstone, 'I have now – to my utter amazement – been assistant secretary of the Albany Club a whole week.'

'Time does fly, madam, doesn't it?'

'How long have you been wine steward?'

'Ever since it was only gentlemen who drank wine, madam.'

'I see. Then you must have known Mr Smallove since he was elected a member?'

Brindles nodded. 'A very nice gentleman, madam.'

Miss Frobisher was puzzled. 'But Brindles, how can you tell? Though Mr Smallove's in the club from morning to night, he never says anything.'

'A member doesn't have to open his mouth to show he's a proper gentleman,' Brindles enlightened her. 'It's how he carries on that counts. Mr Smallove is a very clubbable man, as Dr Johnson said about Mr Boswell, madam. Now, Mr Thackeray–'

Brindles indicated the fearsome portrait of William Makepeace.

'He must have been a very nice member of the club, madam. All the gentlemen in his books spend a lot of their time in their clubs. I always say, a gentleman's club is a gentleman's home, without the inconveniences of domesticity.'

Miss Frobisher stared, amazed.

'You're very literary, Brindles.'

'You'd be surprised what you pick up, madam, listening to forty years of the members' conversation.'

He returned to polishing the glasses.

Miss Frobisher ascended the spiral stone staircase beside the porter's box, which above the library became transmuted into an iron spiral staircase, ending in a bleak corridor illuminated with dusty portraits of forgotten members leading to the club office.

The nerve-centre of the Albany was a poky, sloping-ceilinged room strewn with papers, containing an ancient safe and outmoded typewriter, and decorated with long photographs of past club banquets, taken before the soup with the dinner-jacketed members in a condition of painful sobriety.

While Miss Frobisher climbed the hazardous iron steps, the Gallant Winco was answering the telephone on his roll-topped desk.

'Browne.'

His face lit.

'Bonzo! How are you? Long time no see. What? Your box at Ascot? Love to! Today? Yes, I know it's short notice,' he agreed accommodatingly, 'but that pal of yours didn't know he was actually going to cop a heart attack for the Royal Hunt Cup, did he? Hell!' he added crossly. 'It's a bloody committee meeting this afternoon.'

The Gallant Winco looked round shiftily.

'No, I'll fix it. Piece of cake. Jolly good! Be there for the first race. Cheer-ho.'

Miss Frobisher entered.

'Something wrong?' she cried.

The Gallant Winco sat in his padded swivel-chair with an expression of grief.

'Bad news, I'm afraid,' he admitted. 'Bonzo – old pal of mine, same squadron, the absolute salt – died of a heart attack last week.'

The gruff and Gallant Winco brushed aside a tear with the back of his hand.

'I dunno, everyone seems to get 'em,' he decided gloomily. 'It's like the measles of middle age. Just had the widow on the phone. Shattered, poor darling. Funeral this afternoon. Absolutely got to go.'

'Of course you must go, Wing Commander,' Miss Frobisher told him tenderly. 'I *am* sorry. Such a sad price for old friendship, isn't it?'

'Poor old Bonzo!' The Gallant Winco looked in danger of blubbing. 'Had some great times together. Never forget when we had to hide under a couple of WAAFs beds one New Year's Eve in Hamburg. You'll have to take this afternoon's committee meeting.'

Miss Frobisher was horrorstruck.

'Me?'

The Gallant Winco was surprised.

'Why not? You're the assistant club secretary. Second-in-command should always stand ready to take over at a moment's notice.'

'But I'm female!' she raised the objection.

'What's that got to do with it?' he demanded stuffily. 'Women can do everything that men do these days, except grow long beards. It's in all the newspapers.'

He was already changing his RAF tie for a crumpled black one handy in his desk drawer.

'Keep this for members' memorial services,' he explained. 'One a week during the winter. Heart attacks. You can stand in for me at a few of them, too,' he invited. 'They get dreadfully boring. Like some of the members, who keep on telling the same old stories.'

'But Wing Commander!' continued Miss Frobisher, distraught. 'You know the committee only appointed me because they thought they should keep up with the times. They don't mind my organizing the lunch and the loo paper, but they surely think only a gentleman should be the receptacle of gentlemanly secrets?'

'Oh, the committee's a bit of an outing for its members,' he comforted her. 'They arrive for lunch and a few jars, and doze till it's time to direct the club's destiny at five.' He nodded towards a stack of files and ledgers on the small fridge with ice for his pinkers. 'Minutes and agenda over there.'

'Wing Commander!' Miss Frobisher cried, picking up a letter topping the pile. 'The club's in a state of crisis.'

'Oh? Really? Is it?' he enquired, taking advantage of her turned back to pocket race-glasses from another drawer.

'This letter from the bank manager.' She flourished it. 'They can make the club bankrupt any morning they feel like it.'

He reassured her. 'Oh, the committee'll deal with that sort of thing. That's what the committee's for. Well, good luck. Must get to the church on time.'

He left.

2

The committee of the Albany Club met on steak and kidney pie day.

Lunchtime was convivial, the thirty-odd committee members being the most clubbable gentlemen in the club.

'Do you know what old Thackeray out there said?' enquired George, flourishing his tankard of champers under Lord Curzon's nose, beside my accustomed perch on the bum-warmer.

'He said: "Shakespeare and Raphael never invented anything to equal champagne and oysters at 5.30 on a hot day." Which marks him as a most sensibly sensuous typical London clubman.'

All members of the Albany were impressed by his literary comparison – the first time they heard it. George's stories are as comfortably familiar as the club menu.

'Of course, you realize the club is flat broke? Broke as a church mouse,' Willi cheerfully informed the crowded morning room.

He sat with his pre-lunch tankard of champers, tearing open his pile of letters always awaiting in the porter's lodge, which – as he protested loudly were not about business – the members assumed to come from his mistresses.

He asked Bertie: 'Did you read the committee's report and accounts?'

'Can't understand accounts,' replied Bertie, being a gentleman.

'Well, you can take it from me we're up to our necks in the red.'

'Doesn't seem to do us any harm. Brindles! Another pinkers, and a champers for Mr Smith,' he nodded in Willi's direction.

Willi had taken an English name soon after arrival from over the bright blue Danube, his own having too many zs and umlauts in it to attract the confidence of the natives.

'The day of reckoning must come.' Willi's broad brow gathered thunderously. 'Sure as night follows day, and vice versa.'

'Aren't all London clubs as fashionably in debt as Regency bucks?' suggested Bertie. 'It never seems to matter.'

Rollo joined them with gin and ginger beer, contributing a sparkle of economics: 'After all, we have an unpayable National Debt, but nobody seems to lose any sleep over it, from the Prime Minister down.'

'Mark my words, boys. We may arrive at the club to find the bar full of bailiffs.'

Bertie smiled. 'You're like those chaps with long beards who walk about waving placards saying: "Prepare to Meet thy Doom".'

Willi told him gravely: 'I'm not just trying to make your flesh creep, like the fat girl.'

Brindles refilled his tankard.

'Luckily, I have a little scheme, which I am putting today to the club,' he said mysteriously. 'Cheers!'

'Cheers.'

'I'm the owner of several banks and financial adviser to numerous governments, but you don't seem to want me on the committee,' he mentioned, with the hearty jollity with which, he had learned, English gentlemen express their most fervent desires.

'It's easier for some gentlemen to get into the House of Lords than on to the Albany committee,' Bertie said pointedly.

Willi's eyes flashed. 'So! You mean, I am trying to organize myself into the House of Lords?'

'I'm only pulling your leg,' Bertie replied wearily.

'You had better try the other one. It's got knobs on.'

'Surely, getting into the House of Lords is an ambition

as harmless as wanting to get into Madame Tussaud's?' suggested George.

The Gallant Winco appeared hurriedly from the hall with a fat man in a bow tie and a check suit. 'Might I introduce – damn it! Names go so quickly these days.'

'Spiremaker. Joe Spiremaker.

'From the Liberty Club in New York.'

The Albany was continually refreshed and educated by 'reciprocal clubs' all round the world.

The Opossum Club in Sydney sent members who surprised us by not wearing corks dangling from their hats and drinking beer out of tins.

We learned much about the 'Third World' from members of the Palm Tree Club in Lagos, who neither performed black magic in the bar, nor ordered human flesh in the coffee room.

Members of the Champs-Elysées Club displayed traditional French politeness by inventing ingenious excuses to avoid eating the club food.

No clubmen are more earnestly clubbable than American clubmen.

'Know the Liberty well,' exclaimed Aubrey, who had drifted across. 'Often there, when I had a fortnight in New York.'

'Didn't I hear, they now admit lady members?' murmured George.

'Wouldn't know. Even if they admit lady visitors. I'd packed Gloria off to Cannes.'

'Ah.'

'Have a drink,' Aubrey invited the stranger. 'A bloody Mary or Manhattan, I expect?'

'I'd like nothing better than one of your pink gins,' he accepted quietly.

'How civilized of you,' Aubrey congratulated him. 'Brindles! And one for the Gallant Winco.'

'I esteem it a great privilege to be here in the Albany Club, of which we hear so much back home.'

'That lovely basement bar at the Liberty, with the shutter in the door,' Aubrey recalled. 'Relic of your speakeasy days. You expect Al Capone to push in any moment.'

'I guess the only gangsters we've got as members are Wall Street ones, who wear better clothes.'

'May I talk business?' the American asked, when his pinkers arrived.

Everyone looked appalled.

'I have been asked by the committee of the Liberty if we could make a donation to the Albany Club – maybe fifty thousand dollars – to express our appreciation of the kind hospitality you afford our members travelling to the United Kingdom.'

Everyone looked delighted.

'Any more at home like you?' enquired Willi jovially.

'I guess we can settle the details pretty easily. Meanwhile, can I write a cheque while I'm here?'

'No trouble,' the Gallant Winco told him. 'Limit of couple of hundred quid a day, same as the other members.' He gulped his pinkers. 'Sorry – must rush.'

'You've your memorial service tie on, Winco,' George noticed.

'Funeral. Old pal.'

'Then why've you got your race-glasses?'

'Mark of respect. Was a bookie.'

Brindles struck the gong.

'Hope you like steak and kidney pie?' Aubrey suggested to the visitor, more doubtfully than hospitably.

3

The chairman of the Albany Club was Lord Cotswold, bulgy in eye, stomach, cheek and moustache.

'I have to take the committee meeting this afternoon,' Miss Frobisher apologized anxiously, arriving at five o'clock in the club library with files and ledgers. 'The poor Wing Commander must attend the funeral of a dear friend.'

'The mortality of the Gallant Winco's relations and friends during Ascot Week is most tragic,' sympathized Lord Cotswold.

The first Wednesday of every month, Lord Cotswold presided courteously over the gentlemen at the long library table, furnished with virginal blotting paper, claret-covered rule books and needle-sharp pencils.

Rosie served some with a pot of tea and anchovy toast. Others decided that between lunch and dinner they needed refuelling by Brindles with a whisky and soda.

On a side table between the busts of Sophocles and Walter Scott stood the frightening row of half-dozen walnut ballot boxes, one for each candidate, a hole to hide the hand projecting its wooden ball into the side 'Yes' or 'No', so scattering elation or humiliation, though some shaky-fingered members of the committee brought to it the sporty uncertainty of 'bingo'.

The day's candidates being worthily nondescript, all were elected.

The Gallant Winco's minutes of the last meeting were unanimously approved.

The Suggestion Book was examined. It was decided not to instal a pair of budgerigars to brighten the morning room, nor to instruct the head porter to burn on the club steps a copy of *Private Eye*, which had recently made disrepectful mention of a distinguished member, though the notion of stewed onions on Tuesdays with the sausage and mash was referred for consideration by the kitchen committee.

The next item was 'Conduct of a Member', which within the club emitted the majestically threatening ring of 'Bill of Attainder' in the reign of Henry VIII.

Elderly gentlemen go ga-ga, embarrassing fellow members by imagining themselves the King of Siam, or by total failure to adjust their dress before leaving the bog.

Inept or perfidious gentlemen go bankrupt, ceasing to be members mercilessly *ipso facto*.

One such gentleman in addition hanged himself in a niche of the library, and not being discovered until he was as high as a toothsome grouse, got on the front pages of the newspapers and was considered posthumously to have brought the club into disrepute.

Members continually forgot to return books borrowed from the library, or umbrellas on wet days from the hall stand, but these were thought matters which no gentleman could be expected to keep in mind.

Lord Cotswold looked mystified.

'It appears to be the conduct of a member's wife?'

Miss Frobisher nodded. 'Another member complained that she wrote to his own wife on club writing paper.'

Amazed cries of 'No!' from the table.

'Further, she repeatedly refers to the Albany as "My club".'

'Disgraceful!' muttered the committee.

Old Percy, who claims to remember when a pinkers cost fourpence, decided: 'It was a great mistake, Cotters, ever to let lady guests into the place at all.'

'Hear, hear!'

Lord Cotswold gave a gentlemanly reproof. 'We have invited them, and we must tolerate them. Through thick and thin. It's like marriage. Remind the chap of rule whatever it is, Miss Frobisher, about pinching club property, whether it's the morning-room sofa or a couple of envelopes.'

Old Cecil, who claims to remember the grand Club Dinner for King Edward VII to celebrate the Entente Cordiale, or perhaps it was for King Edward VIII to celebrate his Abdication, piped up: 'Cotters – to paraphrase a motion passed by the House of Commons in 1780 – the influence of ladies in the club has increased, is increasing, and ought to be diminished.'

'Hear, hear,' muttered the committee.

Miss Frobisher sat upright.

'Lord Cotswold, this is becoming embarrassing for me,' she said crisply. 'Would you prefer I left the meeting?'

'No, no!' cried the committee, ashamed of themselves.

'After all, this is a *gentlemen's* club,' persisted Percy.

'And all this feminism nonsense only a passing craze,' Cecil supported him. 'Like vegetarianism.'

Lord Cotswold was a perfect gentleman. 'We are very fortunate to have Miss Frobisher,' he said freezingly. 'She has great experience of catering, and is a charming lady from an excellent family. To extinguish any remaining doubts, I propose from the chair a vote of total confidence in our new assistant secretary.'

'Hear, hear!' cried the committee, remembering that they were gentlemen.

Miss Frobisher suddenly wanted to blub.

'Thank you . . . thank you, gentlemen,' she muttered gratefully, staring mistily into her agenda.

'Any other business?' asked Lord Cotswold briskly.

'Nothing, Lord Cotswold. Except this proposal from Mr Smith.'

'Which Mr Smith?' asked Percy.

'Willi. Villi,' answered Cecil scornfully.

'Well, let's hear what the chap's got to say,' invited Lord Cotswold fairly.

Miss Frobisher scanned the typescript. 'That we sell

the club for an office block, and rebuild it on the top floors. It would give us a wonderful view of St James's Park.'

The amazement was even greater than at members' wives vandalizing the club writing paper.

'The Royal Thames Yacht and the Beefsteak have already done the same,' Miss Frobisher mentioned helpfully. 'We should have all sorts of modern conveniences, like lifts.'

'Too old to start finding my way round a new place,' Lord Cotswold dismissed the idea.

'We'd become like the Chauffeurs' Arms,' Aubrey contemptuously denoted the comfortable RAC along Pall Mall.

'Squash courts, swimming bath and saunas, I suppose?' George said scathingly. 'Such intolerable discomforts should be confined where they belong, on health farms.'

'And we'd be London waifs for years,' Aubrey objected.

Miss Frobisher remarked: 'I believe the Athenaeum would give us hospitality. They have an excellent cuisine.'

George was puzzled. 'The Athenaeum? I thought they had meals on wheels?'

'It would be like shedding your skin,' Lord Cotswold decided gravely.

Everyone agreed the idea as unworkable as rebuilding Buckingham Palace over a supermarket.

'There's just one snag, Lord Cotswold,' Miss Frobisher cautioned. 'The bank is being extremely threatening about our overdraft. They could make the club bankrupt any morning they feel in the mood. Then presumably we'd all stop being members, *ipso facto*.'

This occasioned less disbelief than derision.

George enquired: 'But if we backed Willi, we'd be rich enough for free claret with our meals in perpetuity? Free meals too, probably.'

Aubrey recalled: 'Aren't we making a million or two from the Rembrandt in the card room, which we sent to Sotheby's?'

Miss Frobisher enlightened him: 'Unluckily, it wasn't by Rembrandt. It doesn't seem to be by anybody.'

George remembered: 'This Yank that's blown in from the Liberty Club. They want to give us thousands of dollars.'

'Stinking rich lot at the Liberty,' Aubrey assured the committee. 'Full of Wall Street analysts, who can send the market up or down depending on whether they blow their noise or fart.'

'It would be only gentlemanly to respond to such generosity,' Lord Cotswold suggested chivalrously and speedily.

'Particularly as a party of American gentlemen are arriving from the Liberty this weekend,' Miss Frobisher reminded him.

Lord Cotswold expressed gentlemanly surprise. 'That's news to me.'

'The Wing Commander had the letter . . . some days ago,' she minimized tactfully.

'Shouldn't we present the Liberty with some club property in return for their donation? Perhaps that gold-mounted off-side rear hoof from Lord Rosebery's favourite hunter?' Lord Cotswold mooted handsomely.

Willi was voted down.

'Don't be over-concerned about the bank,' Lord Cotswold ended politely. 'I'm having the chairman fishing my water on the Spey all next week. I declare the meeting terminated. Ah! The bar's open.'

4

'Tripe and onions! It must be Thursday.'

Sniffing the backstairs' aroma, George appeared round Mr Gladstone.

'Brindles! Pinkers!'

'Very good, sir.'

The morning room was as animated as Regent's Park monkey-house before feeding-time.

The committee secrets had as usual circulated round the club with the preprandial rounds of pinkers.

The hot-blooded younger members – under sixty – favoured Willi's plan. Wiser and greyer heads wagged against it.

Willi himself was complaining morosely over his tankard of champers: 'I feel I am aboard the *Titanic*, the night it sank with the band playing *Rule Britannia*.'

'It wasn't *Rule Britannia*, Willi,' Rollo corrected him. 'It was *Abide With Me*, everyone knows that.'

'No it wasn't,' Bertie complained. 'They played *Alexander's Ragtime Band*. I happen to know, because both my grandparents went down in it.'

'How interesting,' Aubrey complimented him. 'My own grandparents luckily had to cancel their cabin at the last moment, because my father got chickenpox. We've still got the tickets somewhere at home.'

Old Cecil stated: 'It was *Nearer My God to Thee*, if the thing actually did sink to music.'

'My grandparents went down in a sailing ship,' contributed Old Percy.

Willi loudly thumped his chair.

'I am not talking about the bloody *Titanic*. I am talking about stopping the club being shut overnight, like some sleazy Soho clip-joint.

A frustration for serious club conversationalists is the preference of members to splash playfully away in puddles, rather than breast the flowing stream.

Further, their ancestors will have left eyewitness accounts of worthy participation in any historical event mentioned, from the Battle of Britain back to that of Hastings.

'Now Willi's having a paddy,' observed Bertie reprovingly.

'I have another plan,' Willi persisted, dogged for the good of the club. 'We shall invite the Duke of Lincolnshire to be patron of the Albany. After all, the job's been vacant since the Marquis of Claymore fell off the Matterhorn.'

George exclaimed: 'Splendid idea! A gentlemen's club can never have too many dukes.'

Contrariwise, Aubrey groaned loudly. 'Not old loony Linkers!'

Willi argued powerfully: 'He is royalty. Surely, no English firm would make us bankrupt if we were related to the Queen? It would be dreadfully bad form. And he'd be tickled pink. I happen to know his Grace well,' he imparted with gentlemanly modesty.

Rollo contributed gloomily: 'Linkers is so balmy, he'd be blackballed at a funny farm.'

'Plenty of royals have been mad,' George said encouragingly. 'Duke of Clarence, George III and so on. It's not particularly troublesome, they always go round with lots of attendants.'

'We'll have a big dinner for him!' exclaimed Willi persuasively. 'With the club's Coronation claret. It will be fun.'

'Might I invite you gentlemen to enjoy your famous Coronation claret this lunch?' mentioned our guest Joe Spiremaker, sitting quietly at the writing desk. 'A few bottles, with the compliments of the Liberty Club.'

George agreed. 'It's a beautifully matured wine. The members can't afford to drink it.'

'I guess it's OK to write another cheque?' Spiremaker enquired mildly. 'London's a terrible temptation for shopping.'

'I'm sure you'll find the Gallant Winco most accommodating,' Aubrey assured him.

'You know the club's gone broke, Brindles?' asked George, as his pinkers arrived.

'It always does, sir, at this time of the year.'

Willi put to him: 'Supposing we sold the club, Brindles, and built a lovely new one?'

'Oh, that would never do, sir!' Brindles was shocked. 'The club is my home, too, sir.'

Aubrey glanced up from the evening paper, brought to the morning room by Hawkins. 'How long have you been living up there in the attics, Brindles?'

'I think ever since they stopped sounding the air-raid sirens, sir.'

George was curious. 'Haven't you ever wanted your own front door, Brindles?'

'Oh, no, sir. I love the club, sir. I've my own little room, and my own little things. The members have been very kind, sir, with mementos. I've Sir Winston Churchill's cigar-cutter and Sir Robert Helpmann's tights.

'There you are, Willi,' George pronounced conclusively. 'Can't possibly sell the club. It would upset Brindles.'

Aubrey exploded.

'Look at this!'

He flourished the evening paper.

'"A Club Divided",' he read angrily. 'In their beastly gossip column. Listen – "I hear that the Albany, the gentlemen's club in St James's, is up for sale. The Albany – motto *Convivium Cum Cerebrum* – is said to enjoy a bank overdraft bigger than some South American banana republics. The idea is disposal of its desirable property for an office block, with the club in the penthouse. A fierce argument has broken out, to sell or not the crumbling Victorian eyesore in Pall Mall. As the deal would put enough millions in the club kitty to keep the members in free port and claret for life, I doubt we have heard the last of this most ungentlemanly row." Disgraceful!' Aubrey hurled the paper across the morning room.

'Willi,' Rollo indicated accusingly. 'That's your bloody paper.'

'Boys, boys, I know absolutely nothing about it,' Willi protested uncomfortably. 'I own a dozen newspapers, television stations, publishing houses,' he explained. 'How can I possibly tell all my employees what to put in and what not to put in?'

'A likely story,' sneered Rollo.

'Honestly, the man who wrote that would not even know I was a member of the Albany,' Willi floundered.

'Rotten sneak,' charged Aubrey.

'Always said, dreadful mistake electing these Grub Street fellers,' Old Cecil informed the morning room.

'I'm going to have a pee,' said Willi, making for Mr Gladstone.

'If you ask me, this is a resigning matter,' continued Aubrey indignantly behind him.

'If you ask me, a debagging matter,' enlarged Rollo.

'Always said, dreadful mistake electing these European fellers,' added Old Cecil.

'Brindles,' said George helpfully. 'Pinkers. All round.'

Miss Frobisher found the Gallant Winco at his roll-topped desk in the office, reading the *Sporting Life*.

'Wing Commander,' she announced. 'There's another cheque from Mr Spiremaker.'

'Mr who?' he demanded gruffly.

'Spiremaker. The man who wants to give us lots of dollars. It's for two hundred pounds again.'

'Names do go so damn quickly these days,' he complained. 'Better give it him.' He nodded towards the safe. 'The chap's perfectly entitled to it.'

Miss Frobisher picked a red and white booklet from papers piled on the fridge.

'I couldn't find Mr Spiremaker's name in the members' list of the Liberty Club.'

'Looked him up, did you?' The Gallant Winco seemed surprised at such curiosity. He took the list from her. 'Probably been elected since. This is fifteen years old,' he indicated.

She suggested gently: 'Shouldn't we send for another one?'

'Suppose so,' he agreed. 'But writing letters is such a bore.' He handed her the *Sporting Life*. 'Better put that back in the morning room. The members might want to read it.'

Descending the spiral stone stairs with the newspaper and the banknotes, Miss Frobisher found Hawkins by the front door.

'There's a busload of members from the Liberty Club in New York arriving for lunch tomorrow,' she instructed him. 'Just direct them to the morning room, please.'

'Very good, madam. Mr Smith –' the porter broke off. 'Your Rolls-Royce just phoned, sir. It'll be a few minutes late.'

'What's the matter, Mr Smith?' Miss Frobisher cried. 'You look awfully miserable.'

'The boys want me to leave the club,' Willi mumbled.

'But what on earth for?' she exclaimed.

'They think I put something about the club in the papers. I didn't. My life is ruined.'

'But Mr Smith!' she consoled him. 'You have so many other interests.'

'But this is the only place in the world where I am a gentleman among gentlemen,' he told her tragically. 'It's terrible.'

'Poor Mr Smith!'

His dark, moist eyes stared solemnly.

'You are quite the most sympathetic lady I have ever met, on either side of the Iron Curtain.'

'Perhaps it's because I'm a vicar's daughter?' she suggested modestly.

'My car,' he announced. He turned back from the front door. 'If ever you want a job on TV, let me know.'

5

'Friday,' said George, sniffing while crossing the chess-board hall the next morning. 'Kipper day'.

He rounded Mr Gladstone and entered the bog.

'Morning Herbert!' he greeted, joining him at the splendid urinals.

'There's been some talk in the club about some item in the newspapers,' Herbert observed quietly.

'Disgraceful affair!' agreed George indignantly. 'Like having your home bugged by the Secret Service.'

'They wonder who did it.'

'Willi did it.'

'Willi didn't do it.'

'Who did then?'

'I did it.'

George stood aghast at the marble.

'I've a young granddaughter,' Herbert revealed calmly, crossing to the marble-girt washbasins, the gilt-edged mirror, the huckaback hand towels and communal hairbrushes.

'A pretty little thing, believe you me. She works on what they call Fleet Street. Wanted to give the gel a bit of a hand.'

'Herbert! I'm ashamed of you.'

'I'm not ashamed,' he assured George impassively. 'Not a bit. Everyone sees me sitting here all day long, don't take a damn bit of notice of me. I might as well be Lord Curzon's bust. I might as well be the bum-warmer. Thought I'd get my own back, just for once. Won't tell a soul, will you?' he asked confidently.

Herbert brushed his thin grey hair.

'I could be someone sitting in a railway carriage,' he complained. 'They never say: "Herbert, you look off-colour today." Or: "Herbert, when's your birthday?" Or: "Herbert, how's the wife and family?" Or even: "Herbert, what'll you have to drink?"'

'Herbert, what'll you have to drink?'

'Champagne. And not that club economy stuff. It's undrinkable.'

'It shall be Bollinger,' promised George.

As Brindles popped the cork under the nose of Lord Curzon, the Gallant Winco appeared in the morning room.

'Could do with a glass of that,' he declared. 'Had a trying morning.'

Old Percy looked over *Country Life*. 'Not sanitary inspectors shutting the kitchen again?'

'No. Scotland Yard. That American chappie.'

Old Cecil looked over *The Field*. 'What, the one with all the money from the Liberty Club?'

'Unfortunately not. Imposter. Left unpaid bills, dud cheques. All round the club. All round London. Club references, of course. He specialized in that sort of thing, apparently. Well known to the police. They say clubs are frightful mugs for the gentlemanly sort of con man.'

'What about those dollars we're getting?' George demanded, Brindles returning with another silver tankard.

'Har! I'll look for that next time I see a rainbow in the sky. Hope you chaps enjoyed the Coronation claret,' the Gallant Winco remembered. 'Because now you've got to pay for it. Furthermore, the rotter's gone off with Lord Rosebery's hoof. Morning, Aubrey.'

'Seen this in the evening paper?' asked Aubrey angrily, flourishing it as he appeared past Mr Gladstone.

'Have a glass of the '78 Bollinger,' George interrupted him.

'The '78! I say.'

'Another bottle, Brindles,' George instructed.

'Very good, sir.'

'This sniggering gossip column. Being funny over asking that dotty Duke to become our patron.'

'Next committee, I'm going to have Willi hounded out of the club,' Old Percy threatened fiercely.

'Willi had nothing to do with it,' George assured him.

'Who did, then?'

'Shan't tell. But if Willi resigns from the club, I do.'

The argument collapsed. Gentlemen in clubs are pathetically susceptible to blackmail.

'The papers'll have even more fun tomorrow,' George predicted cheerfully. 'Now we've been swindled by this crook Spiremaker.'

'Crook?' Aubrey cried. 'But he borrowed a thousand quid off me, to invest in claret for the club.'

The morning room roared. It was the funniest club joke since Disraeli slid down the bannisters again after buying the Suez Canal, but fell off.

'Oh, Wing Commander–'

Miss Frobisher was at Mr Gladstone's elbow.

'Lord Cotswold just phoned. He said not to worry about the bank. He's already had a word with its chairman. And the salmon fishing on the Spey looks excellent.'

'Bank? Rather forgotten about all that.' The Gallant Winco raised his tankard. 'Splendid! No more worries, then? Cheers!'

'Cheers!' agreed George and Aubrey.

They froze, like the look-outs aboard the *Titanic*, with which so many members enjoyed a family connection.

A lady had wandered into the morning room.

And another.

Lady after lady.

'Sure, it's quaint,' said one, looking round unimpressed, unabashed, unashamed.

'You know you're in London, don't you?' agreed another condescendingly.

'This is just how I always imagined the inside of Buckingham Palace to look like,' suggested another.

'Can't we get a drink?' complained another. 'Waiter!'

Miss Frobisher was the first to regain speech. 'Can I help you, madam?'

'Oh, thank you,' responded the first lady amiably.

'We're here for a fortnight, from the Liberty Club in New York.'

'But you're female!' declared the outraged and Gallant Winco.

'Well, sir, so are about half the human race,' she pointed out politely.

'But this is a *gentlemen's* club,' protested Aubrey.

'You mean, you don't have mixed clubs over here?' enquired another lady, who was er . . . er. 'My! Do you allow mixed bathing?'

'Waiter!' called a fat lady. 'Four rye on the rocks. Do you happen to be a lawyer?' she introduced herself to Old Percy. 'I'd like to meet one. I'm a judge in New York State, and I'm anxious to discuss various points in the American and British Constitution.'

Old Percy shook.

'Is anyone a stockbroker?' invited a thin lady. 'I'm a market analyst on Wall Street, and–'

Brindles struck the gong.

'Not only ladies–' gasped Old Percy.

'But intellectual ladies,' shuddered Old Cecil.

'Winco!' demanded George sternly. 'Why didn't you find half the Liberty wore knickers?'

'Sorry,' he mumbled. 'Possibly forgot to post the letter.'

Aubrey drew George urgently aside. 'I say, old man,' he muttered earnestly. 'I do hope this isn't going to get into the papers?'

THREE

1

'Madam!'

Hawkins glared, at his most dauntingly disdainful. It was Wednesday, steak and kidney pie day.

'Can I help you, madam?'

'I wish to see the secretary,' crisply replied the smart and pretty lady who had just burst flagrantly through the gentlemen's front door.

'Have you an appointment, madam?' Hawkins remained astringently aloof.

'No. But my message is so vitally important he will be unutterably grateful for my calling.'

'What name, madam?'

'Jane Christie. Ms. MP.'

Hawkins picked up the club telephone.

'Toby! And Jim!'

Ms Jane Christie MP enthusiastically greeted the two gentlemen arriving for lunch.

'Surely, Jim, they don't elect Socialist MPs to this club?'

'Exactly as they do to the club we're all three members of,' Jim Sharpe told her, in his Yorkshire accent. 'The one that serves nice teas on the terrace beside the Thames.'

'The secretary will see you, madam,' conceded Hawkins. 'Might I respectfully request you use the ladies' entrance?'

'And might I respectfully request you to go and get lost?' she replied sweetly.

'Brindles'll show the way, Jane,' Toby Jeavons invited his fellow Tory MP. 'Then get us a drink, Brindles. Pinkers.'

'And a scotch on the rocks,' said Jim.

'I'd have thought, with your constituency, you'd drink Yorkshire stingo?' Jane suggested.

'Can't stand the muck,' confessed the representative of prideful miners, cricketers and choralists.

Brindles led the lady intruder up the stone and then iron spiral staircase, apologizing solicitously: 'It's a bit awkward, madam. Sir Winston Churchill took a nasty tumble down it when he missed his way after a club dinner.'

'What do you do?' she asked, with politicians' nosiness.

'The wine steward, madam.'

'A heavy workload, I expect? Do you like it?'

'Oh yes, Madam! After all, it's my club as much as the members', isn't it?'

'What do they pay you?'

'We're not allowed to discuss business in the club, madam. The secretary.'

Brindles opened the office door.

'Well!' exclaimed Jane. 'This is a step in the right direction.'

'I'm Ann Frobisher, the assistant secretary.'

She rose from the paper-strewn roll-topped desk.

'Wing Commander Browne, the secretary, is on leave,' she apologized for the Gallant Winco. 'Do sit down.'

'I expect you know who I am?' asked Jane, with the weary confidence of those who are always on the telly.

'I saw your picture in the papers yesterday.'

'My divorce!' sighed Jane in exasperation. 'Why should the sex lives of MPs and the Royal Family arouse public interest second only to the mating of pandas?'

'A drink?'

Miss Frobisher took a recapped bottle of champers from the office fridge.

'Thank you. The Albany Club recently entertained members of the Liberty Club. Your reciprocal club in

New York. As the Liberty is a mixed club, they suffered the disgrace of being female.'

Perceiving her visitor speedily come to business, Miss Frobisher countered: 'This is a *gentlemen's* club.'

'And after some hysterical transatlantic phone calls, you banished them,' Jane swept on. 'One was an old friend, a Congressperson. Her outrage at the infringement of civic rights made the American Civil War look like family bickering.'

'I'm sorry they were upset,' Miss Frobisher apologized. 'But the Albany *did* stand them a lovely champagne party in the ladies' dining room, to make up.'

'Which won't stop me taking the Albany Club to court under the Sex Discrimination Act,' Jane imparted alarmingly.

'But this is a private social club–'

'Is it?' Jane asked sharply. 'All that salmon, pheasant, port, champagne, I bet it ends up on someone's expense account. Clients delight being entertained in this fusty, snooty atmosphere. The Albany is nothing but a business club, like the Rotary.'

'Talking business is strictly forbidden–'

'As your wine steward has already admonished me,' Jane said impatiently. 'Come, Ms Frobisher! Be realistic. Business is done in gentlemen's clubs, like money-changing in the temple. If you get the Biblical allusion.'

'I *am* a vicar's daughter,' Miss Frobisher tripped her onrush.

'A businesspersons' club excluding women is driving a coach and horses through the law,' the MP pressed on. 'I shall have women admitted, or I shall have the club shut.'

Miss Frobisher sat in shocked silence.

'I can only raise the matter with the committee. At five this afternoon,' she decided.

'Very sensible of you.'

'How's the champagne?'
'Splendid. Krug '79, isn't it?'

2

'Good afternoon, Sir Eliot!'

Hawkins jovially greeted the beef-faced gentleman ascending the front steps at four o'clock.

'Afternoon, Hawkins.'

'Lovely day, sir.'

'An exhausting one. Do you realize, I have handed out eighty-four years of imprisonment?

'Oh dear, sir,' commented Hawkins gravely.

'Brindles!' commanded Mr Justice Flintstone, striding across the chessboard-floored hall. 'My tea. With anchovy toast.'

'Very good, sir.'

'Afternoon, Cotters,' he called cheerfully to Lord Cotswold, entering the morning room. 'Afternoon, George. See you've a new novel out. How's it selling?'

'Unnoticeably,' replied George, flicking through the *Economist* on the bum-warmer.

'I must buy a copy,' Eliot encouraged him. 'When it goes into paperback.'

'Not as good as it was!' grumbled Aubrey, from the leather armchair next to Herbert's beneath Lord Curzon.

He hurled *Punch* across the morning room, nearly overturning Brindles with the judge's tea.

'Brindles, tea and muffins,' ordered Lord Cotswold.

'Very good, my lord.'

'Neither's the Old Bailey as good as it was, believe you me.' Eliot started eating anchovy toast like the condemned man a hearty breakfast.

'This miserable gang I sent down this afternoon, for their squalid rapes and muggings,' he complained, shifting his bulk over his teapot. 'In the old days, the prisoners looked a damn sight more respectable than the jury does now.'

'I was once called for jury service,' observed Aubrey. 'The prisoner's lawyer objected to me. I was wearing an Albany Club tie.'

'Wish they'd restore capital punishment,' said Eliot longingly, munching anchovy toast. 'That really was an occasion! The black cap, the chaplain, your clerk in a frock coat, everyone standing, a hush–'

'A deathly hush,' George elaborated.

'That lovely rigmarole!' Eliot crunched his toast. 'You be taken from hence to a lawful prison,' he pronounced doomfully. 'And thence to a place of execution–'

Munch, munch!

'And that there you be hanged by the neck until you are dead, and that your body be buried within the precincts of the prison within which you shall last have been confined before your execution–'

Crunch, crunch!

'And may the Lord have mercy on your soul, amen.'

He slurped his tea.

'Eliot, could you equally pronounce on ladies becoming members of the club?' Lord Cotswold enquired mildly.

George informed him: 'We're the latest victims of the newspapers' pet Tory MP – Jane Christie.'

'That's what gentlemen's clubs are for,' Eliot judged. 'Escaping from ghastly women like that.'

'She's trying to nobble us under the Sex Discrimination Act,' Aubrey said resentfully.

'Ah, the Sex Discrimination Act.' Eliot freed anchovy toast from his back teeth with his forefinger. 'Under Section 29, Subsection 1, it is unlawful to discriminate against women if you offer facilities to the public.'

Lord Cotswold asked optimistically: 'So as chairman, I can reassure the committee this afternoon we're safe, being a private gentlemen's club?'

'On the other hand–' Eliot removed the finger from his teeth and wagged it at Lord Cotswold. 'The Act adds: "or *a section* of the public". Perhaps that describes our membership? Drawn from a section of the public, viz gentlemen. I'd rather enjoy hearing that argued before me by learned counsel,' he declared with relish.

'People are so touchy about their rights these days.' Lord Cotswold sighed. 'Even my ghillies are getting uppish.'

Old Cecil looked over the *Tatler*. 'When I was a young man, if a woman wanted to be liberated I loosened her stays.'

'Brindles!' roared Eliot. 'More anchovy toast!'

At the committee meeting in the library at five o'clock, Miss Frobisher placed the visit from Ms Jane Christie MP top of the agenda. But nobody thought it worth discussing.

The ballot boxes were then invoked, as fatefully as any jury deliberating Mr Justice Flintstone's favourite sentence.

'Mr Rawlings-Smith is elected,' announced Lord Cotswold, Miss Frobisher opening the drawers 'Yes' and 'No'. 'Sir Anthony Goodchild is elected. Professor Devenport is elected.' He reached the fourth box. 'Mr Patel is not elected.'

Lord Cotswold returned to the head of the long library table, Miss Frobisher attentive on his left.

'Gentlemen–'

He looked unaccustomedly embarrassed.

'I don't usually comment on blackballing. It's a matter between members of the committee and their conscience. But Mr Patel is . . . er.'

Old Cecil's shaky voice asked: 'Have we any *legal* obligation to elect members who are . . . er?'

George told him severely: 'We've a *moral* obligation to elect members who are . . . er.'

'We've already decided this afternoon that lady members have no place in the Albany,' Lord Cotswold continued firmly. 'But this is a liberal club, in the widest sense. Gladstone, Disraeli, Churchill, Clem Attlee, all members. It would be doing the decent thing, suggesting to our fellow clubmen in the morning room and the coffee room, that they might consider putting up suitable candidates who are, er, er.'

Silence.

'I take that as approval. Next business, Miss Frobisher?'

'The Suggestion Book, Lord Cotswold.'

She opened the leather-bound volume.

'That soft toilet tissue be provided in the members' bog.'

'You mean, there're different sorts?' Old Cecil was incredulous.

'They even come in delightful pastel shades, old boy,' Aubrey enlightened him.

'Always used the same bum paper since I was at school,' he revealed contemptuously.

'Perhaps members should be offered the choice?' Old Percy suggested helpfully.

'Hard or soft,' nodded Aubrey.

'Like claret or burgundy at dinner,' George amplified.

'See to it, Miss Frobisher, please,' Lord Cotswold escaped from the perplexity.

'Certainly, Lord Cotswold.'

She read from the book: '"That the club should cease taking the *Sun* newspaper. I have frequently noticed, on the first facing page inside, a photograph of an artist's model which might well disturb some of the members".'

The Chairman eyed that morning's *Sun*.

'Seems a strapping gel to me,' he declared.

The paper circulated. Everyone agreed.

'Should *stimulate* some of the members,' Aubrey corrected the suggestion.

'Should stimulate some of the members' memories,' sighed Old Cecil, thinking of ladies' stays.

'We can't censor the naked truth,' decided Lord Cotswold robustly. 'Any other business?'

'We're having trouble with Sir Isaac Newton,' Miss Frobisher told him.

'But he isn't a member,' Lord Cotswold objected.

'His nose fell into Pall Mall this morning. It nearly hit a policeman.'

'Oh, the busts outside the library windows,' perceived George, waving in their direction.

'Been falling to bits for years,' contributed Old Percy. 'Remember when Gainsborough came a purler. Almost killed the editor of *The Times*.'

'Wouldn't it be safer to have them removed?' Lord Cotswold asked sensibly.

Aubrey was outraged. 'Can't do that, Cotters! They're the busts of very famous Englishmen.'

'None of the members has the slightest idea who they are,' added George realistically.

Old Percy grumbled: 'The whole of the club front's a disgrace, if you ask me. Still got some of Charles Dickens's fogs sticking to it.'

'Pity that chap Thackeray frightened him from becoming a member,' reflected Old Cecil.

'Unfortunately, it would cost a fortune to refurbish the club façade,' Lord Cotswold reminded everyone. 'And contrary to public opinion, gentlemen's clubs are miserably poor.'

'Perhaps we should just put up a notice?' said George. '"Beware of Fallen Idols".'

3

The committee descending to the morning room awoke Eliot, snoring loudly under *The Times*.

'Ah! Must be time for a scotch and soda,' he assessed. 'Brindles!'

'And four pinkers,' called Aubrey from the foot of Disraeli's staircase. 'Important committee meeting,' he announced to Herbert and the few other members sitting, reading, dozing or staring. 'Cotters told us we need some, er, ethnic members.'

'Under the Race Relations Act,' Eliot educated him, 'they count as women.'

'You mean, if we're providing facilities,' George pursued this dictum, 'like pink gins, champagne, smoked salmon and grouse – in season, of course – for a section of the public viz gentlemen, we might not be a private club at all?'

'On the one hand, yes,' agreed Eliot. 'On the other, no,' he disagreed. 'I advise you to take counsel's opinion,' he summed up.

'I say!' cried Old Percy, seeing Toby Jeavons and Jim Sharpe strolling from the front door. 'We've got to elect some black chappies.'

'You, Labour MP feller–' Old Cecil pointed shakingly. 'You can put them up.'

Jim looked serious. 'I think I'd like notice of that motion, Cecil.'

'But the Labour Party is surely the guardian of everything decent, honest, fair and proper in our society?' Toby asserted.

'Oh, of course. But I've got to think of my constituency, Toby. Yorkshire's full of working-men's clubs. They're exactly like this, except they have brown ale, dominoes and strippers. And I'd become very unpopular with some of my voters, if I got into the newspapers letting in down here what they want to keep out up there,' Jim revealed with gentlemanly candour.

'It's the British Empire come home to roost.' Eliot raised his glass from Brindle's tray to Kipling's portrait. 'My father took up the white man's burden, you know. He was in the ICS.'

'What's that?' asked Jim innocently.

Eliot was shocked. 'The Indian Civil Service, of course. Doesn't everyone know? I remember as a boy in Poona, we didn't have lunch but tiffin, my father was a burra sahib and drank a burra peg, we sat on the veranda wearing our sola topis, with the punka wallahs toiling inside. . . .'

His voice croaked, drowned in nostalgia.

'The British Empire spread education, the word of God and cleanliness,' affirmed Toby.

Jim had opposing views. 'Come off it! It was a global conspiracy for making money out of the black buggers.'

'Well, that's what we liked to think at the time,' Toby remarked with political dexterity.

'The old British vice of hypocrisy,' Jim accused him.

'It's a frightfully civilized vice. Look at the appalling trouble we get into, when we tell the voters the truth.'

'What do you think, Brindles?' Aubrey asked, draining his pinkers. 'Of black members? Or lady members?'

'I wouldn't mind either, sir, so long as they were gentlemen.'

Aubrey and George shortly went for a pee.

'Aubrey, you're a decent chap,' George stated, as they stood together at the beautiful marble.

'Many in the club seem to think so,' Aubrey agreed modestly.

'I'm going to put up a black member.'

'Can't be anyone I know,' Aubrey reasoned.

'Alhaji Koshoni.'

Aubrey looked blank.

'Don't you read the Sunday papers?' George reproached him. 'Alhaji Koshoni's just written this magnificent novel, *The Moon is Black*. It'll win the Booker Prize, maybe the Nobel. It's all about initiation ceremonies in darkest Africa. You know, trials of manhood and female circumcision.'

Aubrey was baffled. 'How on earth could you do female circumcision?'

'I expect Alhaji Koshoni knows,' George told him easily.

They moved to the washbasins and huckaback hand towels.

'He'd be enormously flattered, put up for the Albany, that goes without saying,' George decided.

'You know the feller?'

'Only by reputation. Which is surely enough? Will you second him?'

Aubrey considered, lathering the Imperial Leather soap. 'I suppose that would be doing the decent thing.'

'Good! We'll have to ask him first, naturally. I'll invite him to lunch. That'll set the cat among the pigeons!' George speculated gleefully.

'Or the crow among the cats,' said Aubrey gloomily.

They moved towards the oak door.

Aubrey frowned deeply. 'Female circumcision. You know, old boy, I just don't get it.'

4

It was Thursday week (tripe and onions day).

Mr Justice Flintstone hurried into the morning room before lunch, looking cheerful despite the melancholy decline of the Old Bailey.

'You've knocked off early, Eliot old boy,' Aubrey greeted him.

'Yes! The chap had the decency to plead guilty. So I gave him a smart twelve years, and toddled off for lunch.' He sniffed loudly. 'I smell tripe and onions miasma ascending the backstairs. Brindles! I feel like a bloody Mary.'

'Very good, Sir Eliot.'

Hawkins appeared at the morning-room door.

'Your luncheon guest has arrived, Mr Gifford.'

George and Aubrey marched towards the chess-board-floored hall.

A huge black man, bulgy-eyed, fat-lipped, hidden from neck to sandals in a vivid, savagely patterned robe, head in multicoloured fez, stood inspecting Thackeray's portrait and whisking a fly-swat.

'I say, old man, let's ask him to the Savoy Grill instead,' said Aubrey.

'You are not going to retreat now,' George told him crossly. He indicated another portrait. 'General Gordon wouldn't like it a bit.'

'But what can I say to the feller?' Aubrey asked wretchedly.

'Just treat him like a perfectly ordinary chap.'

'He'll probably ask in the coffee room for coconut milk and boiled yams.'

'He may ask for Brindle's buttocks spit roast, but we can't back out,' George said impatiently. 'Alhaji Koshoni?'

The visitor flashed brilliant teeth in a big smile.

'My dear chap! You must be George Gifford? Delighted to meet you. I'm an enormous admirer of your books.'

George staggered. The black man was a gentleman.

'This is Aubrey Whitaker,' George said weakly.

'How nice! So charming of you, inviting me to lunch.'

'Been to the Albany before?' George enquired, as they moved towards the morning room.

'Never, dear boy,' Alhaji replied with gentlemanly nonchalance. 'But of course, one knows loads of members.'

'You speak awfully good English,' Aubrey mumbled, bemused.

Their guest laughed heartily. 'Well, one went to Harrow, you know.'

'Do you always go about in those togs?' Aubrey wondered.

'Good Lord, no! I'm only wearing them to promote my book. It's a wheeze of my publisher's. The things one does for one's art!'

He laughed louder.

George ventured: 'A drink before lunch?'

'A pink gin would be super.'

'I never before appreciated the cliché "A cynosure of all eyes",' confessed George, when the three sat at the long coffee-room table after a few pinkers. 'Tripe and onions?'

'I adore tripe and onions.' The guest sniffed and sipped the benison of Brindle's decanter. 'Mmmmm! Gevrey-Chambertin . . . '78?'

George nodded approvingly, adding: 'Brindles! Another bottle.'

'Very good, sir.'

'How's your latest novel selling?' Alhaji asked politely. 'Smashing reviews.'

'Quietly. A lot of people must be buying yours?'

'One must confess so,' Alhaji told him, with gentlemanly modesty.

'Sorry to say, haven't read it,' Aubrey said. 'Ought to buy more books, of course. But after earning a crust all day in the City, simply collapse in front of the beastly box.'

'Didn't George Gissing rather shrewdly decide why people buy books, back in 1903?' Alhaji dissertated, taking a crisp roll from Rosie's basket. 'One, to follow the fashion. Two, to impress the neighbours. To flatter themselves as intellectuals. For cheap presents. And, as he put it: "Those who are merely pleased by the outer aspect of the volume".'

George asked: 'And didn't Somerset Maugham equally shrewdly decide: "If you can give the masses a good thrilling story and let them think at the same time that they are improving their minds you'll make a fortune".'

'*Touché*!' Alhaji laughed. 'Of course, Horace said the same thing: *"Omne tulit punctum qui miscuit utile dulci"*,' he flowered classically. '*"Lectorem delectando pairterque monendo"*.'

'Will you pass the Worcestershire Sauce?' Mr Justice Flintstone asked pointedly, silent across the table during the literary discussion.

George introduced him.

'Charmed,' responded Alhaji. 'I read in the papers, your trying that gang at the Old Bailey.'

Eliot admitted sadly: 'Some thought the sentences too severe.'

'Personally, I thought them too lenient.'

'What a splendid chap!'

'Join us in a glass?' Aubrey invited him.

'Well, I've got the afternoon off.'

'Brindles! Yet another bottle.'

'Very good, sir.'

'Wonder if I might ask, old boy,' Aubrey remembered. 'How would one go about female circumcision?'

Alhaji whispered in his ear.

'I say!' exclaimed Aubrey. 'How extraordinary!'

After lunch, all four moved to the morning room for a decanter or so of Warre's '66.

'Magnificent port, old man!' proclaimed Alhaji, staggering at three o'clock into the chessboard-floored hall with his arms round George's shoulders.

'Mish Frobisher!' exclaimed George. 'Our effishent . . . sharming . . . squse me . . . glamrus . . . assistant secretary,' he managed.

Aubrey introduced the visitor.

'Mr Alha . . . Alaj . . . Koshi something.

'A candidate for the club!' shouted Eliot to passing gentlemen.

'Where's book?' demanded George.

'Here you are, Mr Gifford.' Miss Frobisher opened the thick leatherbound candidates' book on its lectern beside the club notice board.

'Can't find pen,' said George, hand in coat armpit.

'Here you are, Mr Gifford.'

Miss Frobisher smiled kindy, like nanny when the little ones had overeaten.

Something was written in the book.

'You're not going back to the Old Bailey?' Miss Frobisher asked Mr Justice Flintstone in alarm.

'Old Bailey?' he thundered. 'Thank God, no. Ghastly place! Feel I could just tell those drivelling, boring, pompous counsel what I think of them. Also those dim-witted, ill-dressed, smelly-footed jurymen. And those mumbling, rambling, lying witnesses. Not to mention those corrupt, shifty-eyed, brutal policemen. Compared with the other people in court, the criminals are sometimes quite gentlemen.'

He staggered back to the morning room.

'Must have a little nap. Before tea and anchovy toast.'

Hawkins opened the front door.

'Swat that fly!' cried Alhaji, slapping him on the head with his whisk.

The gentlemen thought it all frightfully funny.

'Can I get you a cab, sir?' Hawkins enquired solicitously.

'Get him a rickshaw!' roared Aubrey.

Collapse of stout gentlemen.

5

The club that served nice teas on the terrace offered also ever-open bars.

'Don't often see you in the Strangers' Bar,' said Jim, as Toby wandered in towards ten o'clock one night the following week.

'We call it the Kremlin,' he explained. 'So many of you left-wing MPs lurk in it.'

'The great democracy of thirst,' Jim reflected. He ordered another scotch on the rocks, and the large liqueur brandy Toby thought fitting after dinner.

'I wonder what noble cause Jane Christie is promoting?' Toby wondered, nodding towards her talking animatedly to a tall, pink, ginger, bristly-moustached stranger.

'Herself as usual,' Jim made the ungentlemanly suggestion.

'You know she's trying to shut down the Albany?'

'No!' Jim was horrified.

'Because we won't admit women,' Toby explained. 'Apparently, that's a constitutional outrage second only to the abolition of Habeas Corpus and the repeal of the Magna Carta. In politics, one is always learning something.'

'Women don't understand clubs.'

'Pity. Clubbability is a national asset.'

'You mean, us two are daggers drawn in the Chamber, but we can share a drink, see each other's point of view, and that we're a couple of – well, fairly – normal human beings?'

Toby nodded. 'That's why Britain doesn't keep having revolutions.'

'Unlike foreigners, who haven't the club idea?'

'Foreigners are of course not gentlemen.'

'Had the Germans clubs, Hitler would have been blackballed?'

'Indeed,' Toby assured him. 'Want to join me in a little joke? Putting up Jane Christie for the Albany.'

'Joke?' Jim stared. 'Impossibility.'

'Not at all,' continued Toby smoothly, producing the claret-coloured Club Rule Book.

'Rule No. 1,' he read, sipping his Grande Champagne. '"The Albany Club is founded for social intercourse between the members, regardless of rank, political or religious persuasion, profession, occupation or material wealth. The Club shall consist of members elected by the Committee . . . the members shall enjoy equally the facilities of the Club . . . the members shall not leave the Club premises with unpaid bills . . . the members shall not bring in dogs. . . ." You see, "members".' Toby flicked the Rule Book. 'Not a word about "gentlemen". I've searched carefully, as if going through some controversial Bill before the House. There's nothing to stop ladies being members of the Albany, no more than of the House of Commons. So there.'

Jim grinned. 'What's the idea?'

'One in the eye for George Gifford and Aubrey Whitaker at the club. They're trying to fill the place with black men. You could hardly help noticing that smarmy Old Harrovian they brought to lunch. And think of the publicity – crusaders for women's liberation.'

'That might even spread as far as Yorkshire one day,' Jim reflected.

'Let's flush our bird,' Toby encouraged him, moving across the bar.

'This is General Bickley.' Jane Christie introduced the pair as members of the infamously unfeminine Albany Club. 'One of my constituents. He's a member of White's.'

'Pity a member of White's kicked Nye Bevan down its front steps in 1948,' Jim remembered.

The General smiled. 'Well, Nye Bevan did call the Tory Party "lower than vermin".'

Toby nodded. 'As a Tory MP for many years, I'm sometimes inclined to agree. Jane, Jim and I went to put you up for the Albany.'

'You can't, unless I have some grotesque operation first,' she corrected him.

Toby waved the Rule Book under her nose.

'There's absolutely nothing in this to stop you. The Albany never was a gentlemen's club. No one ever said so. There was no earthly reason why Gladstone and Disraeli shouldn't have enjoyed a glass of port with Florence Nightingale and Charlotte Brontë.'

'Really?' Jane became excited. 'Well! Go ahead. A true blow for freedom. How the newspapers'll love it!'

The division bell ding-donged.

'We must go and vote,' she announced.

'What a wonderful woman!' pronounced the General enthusiastically, the two gentlemen MPs lingering to finish their drinks. 'What a wonderful parliamentarian! One day, she'll be prime minister.'

'Oh God, not another!' said Toby, looking skywards.

6

'Brindles, the club does have the television?' enquired Lord Cotswold, hurrying into the morning room the evening of the following sausage and mash day (Tuesday).

'Oh yes, my lord. In the old bucket and broom cupboard.'

'Thank you, Brindles. And a tankard of champagne.'

'Very good, my lord.'

George and Aubrey were already in the cupboard. So

was Jane Christie, talking to Hector Bullwhistle, familiar in every home.

'My first guest is the lady of whom it is said: "No newspaper would seem complete without." Tireless campaigner against all that is iniquitous, insulting, idiotic in our national life. Everything from shoddy kiddies' shoes to the installation of ladies' loos in the crypt of St Paul's Cathedral.'

Outburst of studio applause.

'Don't see old Hector much in the club these days,' observed Lord Cotswold. 'Getting a bit above himself, I suspect.'

'Jane, you're now taking on a really formidable enemy – the gentlemen's clubs of St James's.'

'Where the country is influenced, perhaps governed,' she told Hector briskly. 'Where businessmen, journalists, politicians, make decisions over extravagant lunches which effect the lives of ordinary decent people.'

The viewers in the bucket and broom cupboard groaned.

'You've said of St James's and its clubs, Jane, "This Bastille on London's bus routes" must be stormed by women?'

'It is as outrageous for men to exclude women from their clubs as from being buried in the same graveyards,' she put it forthrightly. 'I'm up for membership of the Albany – you'll have noticed in the papers. If elected, I shall have made my point and drop my campaign. If not, I have the financial backing of the feminist movement to pursue the Albany Club – under the Sex Discrimination Act – relentlessly through the courts, to the House of Lords and to the European Court of Human Rights into the bargain.'

Applause.

'But would you like it in the Albany?' Hector warned.

'I never asked if I would *like it* in the House of Commons,' she rounded on him. 'To be elected was my duty.'

'Would you make any changes, as a member of the Albany?' Hector enquired.

'Most certainly. Like most men, the members smoke, drink too much, and eat totally unsuitable meals of fats and chips. I should declare the club a smoke-free zone, restrict the sale of alcohol, insist on a healthy diet and install a gym. And as you know,' she threatened zestfully. 'I have a way of getting my own way.'

Aubrey switched the TV off.

'Can't stand that woman in the club, even on television.'

'What are we going to do?' asked George pathetically.

'Elect her,' said Lord Cotswold.

George and Aubrey were horrorstruck.

'I'm calling an emergency committee meeting tomorrow afternoon.'

'But electing that harridan will open the doors to women like the first morning of Harrods sale,' George protested.

Lord Cotswold smiled. 'My dear George – with a female like that in the club, no member in his senses will ever put up another. Thank you, Brindles,' he said as the cupboard door opened. 'And I fancy these gentlemen would like a couple of champers, too.'

In the library at five o'clock the following afternoon (steak and kidney pie day), Lord Cotswold was declaring: 'We have two candidates for election. I would never seek unduly to influence members voting in secret ballot. But we must be realistic, gentlemen. It is unfortunate that Toby and Jim have put up a lady candidate. We know our MPs. If they find a loophole, they drive a gravy train through it.'

'Hear, hear,' came ponderously from the committee.

'If we elect her, as our only lady member, I have confidence that . . . she will remain exactly that. She may tire of teasing us,' he suggested optimistically. 'She may lose her seat in Parliament. She may disappear as a country member and raise chickens. But if we blackball her–'

He paused solemnly.

'She vows to hound us through every court in the land. Nay, the Continent. We could foreseeably end up in the United Nations. That woman is more skilful at making an obnoxious nuisance of herself than a covern of witches.'

'Hear, hear.'

'And she has infinite financial resources. While we – what's the club overdraft, Miss Frobisher?'

'Horrendous, Lord Cotswold.'

'In short, gentlemen, the club would become bankrupt and shut. Shall we vote?'

Old Percy whispered to Old Cecil, taking balloting balls from Miss Frobisher: 'That female will be elected only over my dead body.'

'Which, if I may say so, Percy, for both of us will not be long in arriving,' Old Cecil observed sadly.

'Precisely,' Old Percy agreed stoically. 'That's why I don't give a monkey's rupture what happens to the club in the distant future. Shan't be here. This is a matter of principle. Going to blackball her. Will you join me, to do the job?'

'Splendid idea! It'll be one in the eye for Cotters. Trying to stuff the club with black men. Outrageous.'

'Mr Alhaji Koshoni is elected,' announced Lord Cotswold, opening the drawers.

Silence.

'Ms Jane Christie MP . . . is not elected.'

Cheers, back-slapping, agendas flying in the air.

England could have won the Ashes.

7

Late that evening, George, Aubrey, Toby and Jim were sitting mournfully over a decanter of Warre's '63 in the morning room.

'I'm sorry, chaps. It was just a joke. Which went wrong,' Toby apologized again.

'I don't suppose they actually fell about in Ancient Rome, when Caligula made his famous horse a consul,' said Jim, referring to the animal which trots regularly through Parliament.

'At least we know what we're in for,' George depicted gloomily. 'The bloody woman will sue us. Bankrupt us. Shut us.'

'Then where shall we go for lunch, old boy?' asked Aubrey, dismayed. 'Can't stand restaurants. Get used to having steak and kidney on Wednesday, tripe and onions on Thursday, sausages and mash on Tuesday.'

The long-case clock between Thackeray and General Gordon struck eleven.

'Wonder if both this afternoon's candidates are home yet?' George speculated wearily. 'Better try again, I suppose, phoning the good news and the bad news.'

All four moved to the mahogany telephone box the size of a summerhouse beside the porter's cubicle.

'Hello? Alhaji?' began George. 'Been trying to get you. Congratulations! You've been elected to the Albany.'

'George! I'm terribly, terribly flattered. But I was frightfully drunk when you put me up, and, quite frankly, the Albany isn't my cup of tea. I mean, it is just the weeniest bit stuffy and pompous, isn't it?' the newly elected member suggested with gentlemanly good humour. 'Would you mind awfully if I backed out? But it was a lovely lunch, you must be a guest at my clubs, Annabels, Crockford's, or a most interesting little one in Shepherd's Market. Bye!'

'We've been blackballed,' George informed the others.

Toby phoned.

'Jane?'

'I'm in bed.'

'Sorry. Bad news, I'm afraid. Not elected to the Albany.'

'Oh, dear. What a pity. But I've wonderful news. I'm getting married again.'

'Congratulations.'

'To Major-General Bickley. You know, you met in the Strangers' Bar. I'm dropping my campaign against gentlemen's clubs.'

'What!'

'You see, my future husband won't let me. He says I'd simply incite women to get into White's. And he'd have to resign. Then where would he get his hair cut?'

'You mean, you're submitting to your husband's will?' Toby marvelled.

'Just *you* try doing something the General doesn't want you to. Night, night!'

Toby caught the delighted gurgle of a liberated woman captured between the sheets.

'Jane's decided to torment one gentleman, instead of a whole club of them,' Toby explained simply.

'We're all back to square one?' suggested George.

'Feel a bit miffed,' complained Aubrey. 'Like having a house which nobody thinks worth burgling.'

They wandered back to the morning room.

'Brindles, we're not going to have ladies in the club after all,' Toby told him cheerfully.

'I'm so glad, sir. Ladies are all very well, but with all that fuss, it's a wonder gentlemen don't start campaigning to get into maternity homes, sir.'

'More port!' called George.

'Very good, sir.'

The decanter appeared. They raised their glasses.

'Here's to our male–' started George.

'Chauvinist–' admitted Jim.
'Slightly racist–' murmured Toby.
'But very own–' augmented Aubrey.
'Club!' ended them all.

FOUR

1

On a sultry midsummer morning, George, Aubrey, the Gallant Winco, the Professor and Brindles occupied the morning room, all transfixed with horror.

Their agonized faces recalled the works of Stanley Spencer (never a member, artists are regrettably infrequently gentlemen) for five terrible seconds. Then they dissolved into Halsian jollity.

'He's caught it!' they cried together.

'Right on the bloody boundary!' chortled the Gallant Winco, leaning against the bust of Lord Curzon.

'We've won!' cried the small, bald Professor, applauding wildly from the edge of the bum-warmer.

They were facing a television set, 'patiently and anxiously watching every turn of fate in the game, as if the event had been the meeting of two armies to decide their liberty,' as Rev John Mitford wrote about the Men of Hambledon playing on Broad-Halfpenny Down in *The Gentleman's Magazine* of 1833.

'Brindles!' commanded Aubrey. 'Champers.'

'Very good, sir.'

'Mind if we turn that off?'

Toby had wandered from the hall.

He conceded: 'Though as an MP, I salute the club's sound sense of values. Television allowed in here for the Test Matches. Not for General Elections.'

'We've just won the Ashes,' the Professor enlightened him breathlessly.

'Really?' said Toby indifferently. 'I was a wet-bob,' he added, letting everyone know he was at Eton, as Etonians do.

'Well, your school's been playing cricket against Harrow since 1805,' the Professor countered robustly. 'When Eton lost.'

'What do you expect?' Toby reached for *The Times*. 'With the Harrow captain mad, bad and dangerous to know – Byron.'

'He scored two, bowled,' imparted the Professor, with that cricketer's obsession with minutiae.

'I've published a dozen novels,' George reflected, slouched in his favourite leather armchair. 'And you know the only thing I wished I'd written? The cricket match from A. G. Macdonell's *England, Their England*.'

'Yes! Set in the twenties, wasn't it?' Aubrey recalled warmly.

He considerately switched off the set, now displaying the threatened thundery rain bucketing upon the wicket, while the suave commentator meditated sombrely that the final catch being dropped would have sent every Englishman to bed bitterly frustrated.

George continued dreamily: 'The villagers against the gentlemen from London. On the green, outside the pub. The local hero the blacksmith, bowling in his braces. Beer in its native pewter. Good sportsmanship. Good fellowship. The demonstrable democracy of flannels.'

'Not much sportsmanship about it, I remember,' Aubrey corrected him. 'Both sides were as keen to win as the Kaiser or Hitler.'

The cork popped.

The game bestowed upon the world by a London gentlemen's club (now two centuries' old) exhibits starkly in the sunshine those self-effacing, reluctantly flaunted English virtues of decency, fairness, chivalry, determination, modesty, courtesy, dignity, unpretentiousness, honesty, health, unselfishness, humour, politeness, patriotism, inexcitability, civilization, tenacity, steadfastness, staidness, skilfulness, social cohesion and several other things. Many Englishmen thus profess an enthusiasm for cricket that reflects the game's aura round their own heads.

Toby would have stepped briskly to the crease if selected for the House of Commons annual fixture against the Lords, or for those diverting the Conservative – as the Labour and Trade Union – conferences. Ready participation in such harmless and universally applauded eccentricity brings easy identification of the players as gentlemen, and not the self-seeking, devious rogues that the public, with its irritating shrewdness, suspects them to be.

Aubrey, George, the Gallant Winco displayed towards cricket the clubman's self-indulgent, touching boyishness. The Professor's interest was deep and philosophical, and like genuine enthusiasts for anything he never flinched from boring everyone in sight about it dreadfully.

'My delight, as a professor of physics, is using my lab to study the aerodynamics of the cricket ball.'

The Professor produced one from his pocket, as if any summer's day any gentleman might do the same.

'In a perfectly smooth sphere moving through a non-viscous fluid – gases are of course fluids,' he demonstrated earnestly to George and Aubrey, 'the pressure is lowest where the velocity is highest, on the sides. This is Bernoulli's theorem.'

They nodded sapiently.

'But the raised seam, which you observe here, trips the laminar air into turbulence, so the ball swings to that side . . .'

He continued bafflingly for twenty minutes, until permitting the interruption of Aubrey ordering more champers.

2

Mr Stephen Stallybrass QC was singular among the Albany Club cricket fanatics.

He played it.

Vast, sallow, glossy-haired, mastiff-jowled, the chimes of his eloquence rang in court not to vindicate the innocent or castigate the wicked, but on behalf of multi- million-pound companies in complex tax cases, who fee'd him lavishly for putting the boot up the Inland Revenue.

'What wonderful news!' He strode in striped trousers across the chessboard floor from the front door.

'Yes!' Miss Frobisher was pinning the luncheon menu to the green baize notice board amid announcements of bin- end sales, lost umbrellas and regrets at the deaths of members. 'We won.'

Stephen looked as if she had just delivered a verdict in his favour.

'You're a cricket buff, too? Why, that's even more wonderful news!'

He slipped a black-jacketed arm round Miss Frobisher's shoulders and squeezed her, as an expression of their mutual enthusiasm.

'All morning in court, my clerk was passing me little notes saying how England were getting along. Finally, the judge said very testily: "You might at least let us know the score, Mr Stallybrass".'

Miss Frobisher laughed. He laughed, squeezing her again, as an expression of their mutual enjoyment.

He peered at the menu.

'It's Tuesday. Sausage and mash day. I should have thought a lady assistant secretary might have given us more adventurous menus,' he chided.

'I did try, Mr Stallybrass. I put on cannelloni, moussaka, cassoulet. But the members only complained about the foreign muck.'

'They eat it in restaurants,' he carped indignantly.

'Yes. But members in the club behave quite differently from the way they do outside.'

'I suppose most of us are old enough to be fatherly, eh?'

He squeezed once more, expressing appreciation of a favourite daughter.

The club had come to terms with Miss Frobisher.

Its initial feelings about her – from horror to smug trendiness – were modified by the members' inbred tenderness towards one of the weaker sex.

She had swiftly repaid this by presenting the demure, intelligent charm of a well-educated vicar's daughter, which was reassuring, as unlikely to cause embarrassment by unduly inflaming the members' passions.

'We're very lucky to have you,' Stephen complimented her, squeezing again.

'Thank you, Mr Stallybrass.'

'You're a very nice girl.'

He patted her cheek.

'Thank you, Mr Stallybrass.'

'A very nice girl indeed.'

He patted her posteriors.

'Thank you, Mr Stallybrass.'

He moved with an indulgent smile into the morning room.

'Dirty old bugger,' Miss Frobisher muttered into the notice board.

'Catch!'

The Professor tossed Stephen the cricket ball, which he caught stylishly.

'It's a wonder to me that the club never gets up a team,' Stephen suggested, bouncing the ball towards our richly moulded ceiling with the chandelier which is cleaned every August.

'Why not?' George agreed enthusiastically. 'Surely the charm of this place is being a school without any lessons? Most schools can raise a cricket side.'

Stephen assumed an expression of insufferable modesty.

'Look, I live in a completely unspoiled village in Sussex, where I happen to be captain of the local cricket team.'

The others were rewardingly impressed.

'We've got to scratch next Saturday's fixture – the local theological college has got mumps. Why doesn't the club fill in?' he invited.

He added apologetically: 'It's all terribly rustic, of course. Just a pitch cut among the daisies and buttercups outside the Red Cow. You hit sixes into the horse-pond.'

'Have you a clock which strikes the hours from a flint-towered church?' George enquired eagerly.

'We have, actually.'

'Smoke from red-roofed cottages curling slowly into the golden haze?'

'I expect so.'

'White butterflies flapping their aimless way among the gardens?'

'I'm sure we have.'

'Straight out of *England, Their England*!' George finished quoting jubilantly. 'The game's on.'

'Good! I'll fix everything my end.' Stephen sent the ball back to the Professor. 'I must go wee-wee,' he announced, with the touching artlessness of behaviour seen in nursery schools and gentlemen's clubs.

'You're going to find blacksmiths thin on the ground, George,' Aubrey warned, while Stephen strode purposefully towards Mr Gladstone.

'What matter if they're TV repair men, dear boy? Country people haven't changed since Wisden first took quill to his Almanack.'

'Miss Frobisher–' directed the Gallant Winco, his assistant appearing from the hall with a sheaf of coffee-room menus – the *carte* and the 'ordinary'.

'Notice on the board, please. Members desiring

selection for the club cricket team. It's on Saturday. V. Mr Stallybrass's village.'

'But what a lovely idea! I'll organize an absolutely super picnic.'

'No, no!' George objected. 'That would embarrass our rustic hosts. Just a simple ploughman's lunch, bread and cheese and pickled onions.'

'And hard-boiled eggs,' added Aubrey. 'Whoever heard of a picnic without hard-boiled eggs?'

Miss Frobisher banged the gong.

'One o'clock already!' Toby rose from his armchair.

'I'm being lunched at the Savoy by lobbyists,' he apologised to his fellow-clubmen. 'The Friends of something or other. Or possibly the Antis. I do so loathe pressure groups,' he orated. 'Their objects are inconsequential or incomprehensible, their function the nutrition of self-importance and the intoxication of prejudice.'

'God save us from moralists,' George agreed. 'The bad are so frightfully useful, making others feel so delightfully good.'

'You're playing on Saturday, Toby,' Aubrey told him.

'I'm not!'

'Good for your image. Alec Douglas-Home batted for Middlesex and became prime minister.'

'He's right,' Toby said soulfully, wandering towards the front door with Miss Frobisher. 'The image is all. Though God knows, voting for a politician because he looks honest on television is muddling the poke with the pig.'

'But you looked lovely on *Panorama*, Mr Jeavons,' said Miss Frobisher, like a vicar's daughter who watched only the sensible programmes.

'Did you think so?' He grasped the compliment pathetically. 'How terribly sweet. I think I hate PRO people as much as lobbyists,' he decided. 'You realize, Miss Frobisher, we know more for real of William the Conqueror than of the current American President, who is created like a fictional character in Gore Vidal? Or possibly Zane Grey? And I can't distinguish one of our royal princesses from the other, now they're all told how to look, and what to do, by ad men.'

Toby saluted languidly members arriving for a few pinkers before their sausage and mash.

'How much simpler it was for the Victorians! All the voters saw of a politician was a raucous man in a frock coat going red in the face at the end of a gaslit hall.'

'But Mr Jeavons, you've got the image fit for a future prime minister,' Miss Frobisher consoled him politely.

'Which I'd like to be,' he assured her readily. 'For the good of our country, of course. That's the charm of politics. Identifying your own progress with the nation's. Otherwise, it's a hard life,' he revealed touchingly. 'Trapped in the House of Commons half the night, always voting at your party's call with no thought of thinking for yourself at all, like the chap in *HMS Pinafore*. Indeed, it's like being a passenger aboard some huge liner with twenty-four-hour bars, sailing absolutely nowhere. It wrecks your marriage. My wife has just left me.'

He stopped by the porter's cubicle and looked earnestly into Miss Frobisher's eyes.

'I *am* sorry, Mr Jeavons.'

'It wrecks your health. It saps your mind. Do you know what Bernard Shaw said in 1907? "Alcohol enables Parliament to do things at eleven at night that no sane person would do at eleven in the morning".'

'Perhaps you should play more cricket, Mr Jeavons?'

'Perhaps. Balfour was a golfer and Neville Chamberlain a fly-fisherman,' Toby said wistfully. 'Baldwin was keen on cricket, though Churchill never attempted anything more exerting than bezique. Do you know, you're the most sympathetic person I've ever met?'

'*Am* I?' Miss Frobisher replied in surprise.

'You have a womanliness so rare in the age of feminism.'

'Oh, thank you, Mr Jeavons.'

'How I wish that I were able to enjoy so delightful a personality as an individual, and not a member of a club.'

'Do you, Mr Jeavons?'

'Tell me–'

Toby glanced round. He dropped his voice.

'Do you have a . . . love life?'

Miss Frobisher smiled.

'Isn't that something one never discusses in the club, Mr Jeavons?'

'I suppose so,' he agreed, disconsolately stepping into Pall Mall.

'Randy old sod,' Miss Frobisher muttered into the closing front door.

3

Thursday at the Albany Club was tripe and onions day, which made for a busy lunchtime.

George, Aubrey and the Professor were staring sombrely at the green-baize board in the hall.

A sheet of club writing paper – the embossed club crest depicting a Loaf of Bread, a Flask of Wine and a Book of Verse, with the club motto: *Convivium Cum Cerebrum* – proclaimed the only members presenting themselves for selection in the Club XI as G. Gifford, A. Whitaker, Prof. R. Jeffs and T. Jeavons MP.

'No takers,' George grunted.

'I just can't understand it.' The Professor scratched his bald head. 'It's been my lifetime's belief that inside every Englishman there's a Jack Hobbs struggling to get out.'

The three wandered into the morning room, where Miss Frobisher was arranging a huge bowl of flowers under Lord Curzon's nose.

'Brindles – three pinkers,' Aubrey ordered gloomily.

'Very good, sir.'

George remarked jokily: 'Miss Frobisher, it seems you'll have to play cricket for the club.'

She gave a lovely gasp. 'But Mr Gifford! That would be wonderful. Such an honour.'

Aubrey frowned. 'Can you actually play?'

'Oh, yes! My father made sure of sending me to the right school.'

'Bat or bowl?' enquired George.

'Middle-order bat and leg-spinner. They say I've got a deadly googly,' she commended herself modestly.

'Pity my son isn't a member,' the Professor sighed, taking his pinkers from Brindle's silver tray. 'He's a Cambridge cricket blue.'

'Put him up,' said Aubrey at once. 'We'll call an extraordinary committee meeting and elect him tonight. It's in the rules, you know – gentlemen giving great service to club and country.'

The Professor said sadly: 'That would be the culmination of a life – perhaps not undistinguished – to see my son a member of the club. But alas! He does not take kindly to the suggestion.'

'Why ever not?' George asked unbelievingly.

'He thinks we are a bunch of painfully dreary old fuddy-duddies.'

Miss Frobisher smiled, sticking begonia among floribunda. 'Perhaps membership of the Albany Club should be inherited, like the House of Lords?'

'No, no,' the Professor disagreed. 'It's pure selfishness, wanting a son in the club. Expecting the young to be like us. We're stuffed museum specimens, who would disintegrate rapidly outside our glass case.'

'I haven't got a son,' remarked George. 'Come to think of it, now I haven't even got a wife.'

'Vanessa?' The Professor was alarmed. 'Not dead?'

'No,' said George firmly. 'Gone before. It makes you

appreciate the club enormously. So sympathetic. In any marital row, everyone can be relied upon to take the husband's side.'

Aubrey reached for his pinkers. 'Brindles, do you play cricket?'

'Oh, sir!'

'Care turning out for the club on Saturday?' George invited genially.

'Anything you say, sir.'

He struck the gong.

'What lovely flowers!'

Aubrey had hung about the morning room, the others draining their pinkers and leaving promptly for lunch.

Miss Frobisher told him: 'I thought they'd brighten the club up.'

'Before you came, Miss Frobisher, the club was a pretty bleak place,' he admitted charmingly. 'You're a delightful decoration in yourself.'

'How very kind of you to say so, Mr Whitaker.'

Aubrey came closer.

'Do you live in Town?'

Miss Frobisher continued flower-arranging.

'I've a little flat.'

'Would you let me take you out to dinner one night?' Aubrey explained: 'Just to show my appreciation of all you do for the club.'

Lupin in hand, Miss Frobisher's eye pierced his.

'I think that would come under the heading of gratuities to the staff, Mr Whitaker. Which – as a member of the committee – you well know to be strictly forbidden.'

Aubrey shrugged, snapped off a rose-bud and poked it in his buttonhole.

He asked nonchalantly: 'What happened to that young new member – Harker-Hewitt, wasn't it? – I surprised you kissing in the members' loo?'

'I was in the members' loo, Mr Whitaker, unblocking the drains,' she told him steelily. 'And I happened unexpectedly to meet Mr Harker-Hewitt there after a very long time.'

'Still see him?'

She stood back to admire the bowl. 'If you must know, the occasional phone call.'

'Ah, well,' said Aubrey enigmatically, drifting into the coffee room.

'Bloody brass-arsed cheek,' Miss Frobisher muttered into the flowers.

George appeared round Mr Gladstone.

'Miss Frobisher – I've half a mind putting in the Suggestion Book that you should be added to the club crest,' he revealed chirpily. 'We've already the loaf, the book, the wine, you art the Thou.'

'That wasn't really very witty, Mr Gifford.'

'No, I suppose it wasn't,' George agreed handsomely. 'But I had to concoct some introduction before inviting you to Paris for the weekend.'

She said quietly: 'Fuck off, Mr Gifford.'

'Probably you're quite right,' George conceded. 'I hope the tripe and onions isn't already finished.'

'Quentin, do you play cricket?' Miss Frobisher asked.

Harker-Hewitt rolled back on the pillow of his 'designer' bed in the splendidly interior-decorated bedroom of his flat in Chelsea Mews.

'Play *what*?' he demanded.

'Cricket. You know. A game with a ball, six stumps, two bats and two men in white coats.'

'What a remarkable thing to ask at this particular moment.'

'It occurred to me you could play for the club on Saturday.'

'The club! But I only go there to outrage them. You know, tipping the waiter. Great fun!'

'You are naughty.'

Miss Frobisher made a pattern with her fingertip on Harker-Hewitt's flat tummy.

He recalled indignantly: 'Do you know, just because I'm an interior decorator, they automatically assumed I was a homosexual.'

She assured him softly: 'A lot of them would love to be where you are.'

'Make rude suggestions, do they?' he asked with interest.

'Extremely polite ones.'

He sighed. 'So that's how gentlemen behave? I've often wondered.'

'Gentlemen are complicated. Each uses a different approach. It's very interesting.'

'It's very pathetic.'

She fell silent, doodling round Harker-Hewitt's navel.

'They are perfectly ordinary men, as you'd find staying with their extremely ordinary wives in any holiday hotel. But in the club they behave like a lot of adolescents – oh, very well brought-up adolescents – with the run of the tuck shop.'

'They're a bunch of dirty old members,' he assured her.

'Are you going to play cricket, love?' she wheedled.

'I suppose I must, now you're oiling my bat,' he conceded.

4

Miss Frobisher enjoying also the organizational skills of Snow White among the Seven Dwarfs, marshalled the Albany Club Cricket XI in the chessboard-floored hall after breakfast that Saturday morning, with their bats and bags and simple lunch and cans of Ruddles' Rutland ale (Aubrey had suggested chilled Moselle, but George said that country people regarded wine as fit only for foreigners).

Miss Frobisher had hired a 'minibus', which she drove down the 'motorway' into Sussex.

How well I remember touring Sussex in my roadster, on summer's evenings with the hood folded back on the tonneau! Visiting many a spiffing roadhouse, in days when the 'Highway Code' directed a gig driver to circle his whip overhead to indicate he was making a left, when you cranked your engine into life, when there were no fussy tests for motors or drivers and when you could be blind drunk behind the wheel without anyone bothering.

Our magical countryside still casts a spell beyond these intrusive steel-girt concrete thoroughfares. It entices the motorist along treed roads and hedged lanes into the age I remember of running-boards, tartan rugs, gauntlets and Rowntree's Motoring Chocolate.

The bus reached a rough track behind the promised flint-towered church, which led to a faded sign directing 'Cricket Ground', another underneath warning 'Beware of the bull'.

Through a five-barred gate, they bumped round a field clasped in the gentle bosom of the Downs, sloping towards the ancient Red Cow, a rickety pavilion and nail-spiked scoreboard, which addressed a pitch shorn amid the everyday grass.

'Fantastic!' George gave a wondering sigh. 'This is England – *Their England*.'

The team debouched between pavilion and pub.

It became suddenly and saddeningly clear that the sunlit scene was no more genuine than fairyland in a Christmas toy department.

Behind the Red Cow glittered rows of Rollses, Bentleys, Porsches and Jaguars. Beside it, a marquee with drawn-back flaps displayed lunch tables with white cloths and flowers. Waiters in white jackets and waitresses in black dresses poured champagne and Pimms outside among a gathering dressed for Ascot.

'*We're* the yokels,' muttered George.

Aubrey asked: 'You don't expect someone like Stephen Stallybrass to bowl in his braces, do you?'

Stephen bustled up, beautifully blazered.

'So you managed to find our obscure little village? Congratulations!' he greeted them genially. 'You see, we take our cricket seriously, if life in this nook is simple to the point of quite delightful boredom. Terence is a video buff.'

He indicated a young man pointing a complicated camera at them.

'He's making a record of village life.'

'You'll have to lend us a sub,' George apologized. 'I did a press-gang job in the bar yesterday lunchtime, but we're still short.'

'No trouble,' Stephen told him smoothly. 'There's many a village lad itching to play. Here's my side.'

He produced a typewritten list on paper headed 'The Hall'.

'We have to exchange teams before tossing for innings, as you know,' Stephen continued amiably. 'It's Law One in Wisden. The charm of cricket is the rules applying equally in this unsophisticated cranny as at Lord's, as the law in a magistrates' court or the Old Bailey.'

'Quite,' said George.

The home captain's finger picked out names.

'That's the MD of Base Metals Ltd,' Stephen explained impressively. 'And he's very big in merchant banking. You must have heard of that one – the takeover king.'

'I haven't a list, but you know everybody,' George explained. 'Miss Frobisher's going in third wicket down.'

Stephen's eyes glinted.

'What an accomplished young lady! Her legs will be an embellishment in the slips.'

'Quite,' said George.

'We've even brought a scorer,' Aubrey interrupted. 'You know my wife, Gloria?'

She was busty and gingery, expensively dressed and trimmed.

'Delighted,' Stephen confessed himself. 'Why don't you find a glass of champagne in the tent?'

He turned to the others. 'I'll show you the visiting side's changing room. Rough but adequate.'

The cricketers followed him to a tiny plank-walled room with a bench along one side and splintering lockers on the other, smelling of linseed oil.

'Perhaps I'd better go in here?'

Miss Frobisher disappeared with her Adidas bag through a door marked 'Storeroom'.

Stephen noticed.

He sauntered into the main area of the pavilion, littered with bats, bags and boots, hands clasped behind his back, staring contemplatively heavenwards. He made a calculated pause. He sauntered back. He threw open the storeroom door.

'I say! I really am most frightfully sorry.'

Miss Frobisher was 'topless'. She gave a charming little squeak and covered her nakedness with a cricket-pad.

'I'd no idea that you were in here.'

'That's perfectly all right, Mr Stallybrass.'

'I'm afraid it's not very comfortable.'

'It serves quite well, Mr Stallybrass.'

'You're sure I can't find you better accommodation?'

'Not at all, Mr Stallybrass.'

'Delighted you could come down with the club side, Miss Frobisher.'

'It's a great pleasure, Mr Stallybrass.'

'Thank you, Miss Frobisher.'

'Thank *you*, Mr Stallybrass.'

He shut the door, clasped his hands behind him, and sauntered away staring contemplatively heavenwards.

5

In a net beside the pavilion, Miss Frobisher – dressed delightfully for the Centre Court, plus pads – was cracking hearteningly at the bowling of Harker-Hewitt, in flannels and a Turnbull & Asser pink shirt.

'You actually play cricket?' Aubrey fielded the ball, looking surprised.

'Why not?' Harker-Hewitt looked equally so.

'But you're an interior decorator,' Aubrey explained. 'How remarkable.'

'Brindles, are you sure you can play?' George enquired kindly.

'Oh yes, sir. When I lived at the YMCA, sir, I was considered very hot stuff at cover point.'

Aubrey observed: 'You seem to have grown out of your flannels.'

'Miss Frobisher found them, sir. They're part of the veg cook's uniform.'

The club team had been completed save one by the Gallant Winco, who doubted if his hip would last much more than an over or two in the field.

And by Colonel Chewsett, who had played for the Brigade, always wore a Brigade tie, and like all former Guards officers gave the impression that further achievement in life was superfluous.

And by George's publisher, who had once turned out for the annual match v. The Authors, which has a luncheon interval longer than the hours of play.

The three had gathered attentively round the flannelled Professor, ball in his fingers.

'Spin bowling is tremendously interesting, you know,' he assured them. 'It all depends on the Magnus effect. The bowler uses the seam of the ball as a cogwheel. See? He can spin the ball on an axis parallel to its line of flight, like the turbine of a jet engine.'

The Professor twirled the ball in the air.

'Or at right angles to its line of flight, like a bicycle wheel. Or perpendicular to its line of flight, as if the batsman had a child's humming-top coming at him through the air. Watch.'

With the action of a stealthy crab, the Professor bowled one at Miss Frobisher.

'Who's that feller waving at us?' asked the Gallant Winco.

A slight young man in jeans had left his sporty car among the glistening limousines.

'Why, my son Tom!' exclaimed the Professor delightedly. 'The cricket blue,' he added proudly, Harker-Hewitt and Miss Frobisher joining them. 'He promised he'd try and come along to support us. He's a houseman at Bart's, you know. They have to work terribly hard.'

'Hello, Dad.' Tom grinned. 'Haven't you started yet? Or are you all out already?'

'You're playing,' George directed immediately.

'But I haven't any gear,' he protested. 'Not even an Oliver Cromwell.'

'A what?'

'The protector,' Miss Frobisher explained. 'A box.'

'Borrow mine,' Aubrey offered. 'And I'm sure we can find another pair of chef's trousers.'

Stephen was approaching from the luncheon tent.

'We shan't need a sub,' George informed him happily. 'The Professor's son's turned up.'

Stephen frowned. 'Is he a member of the club?'

'Been a member for years,' the Professor told him indignantly.

'Shall we toss for innings?' Stephen invited George.

'Tails.'

'Hard luck. We'll bat.'

Harker-Hewitt took Stephen by the blazer sleeve.

'Club tradition demands a bet. A monkey to win?'

'Five hundred quid?' Stephen looked dubious. He squared his shoulders. 'Very well. You're on.'

The match would not have excited the pen of the late Neville Cardus, a member of the Albany who kept us spellbound in the bar equally about cricket and concerts.

Brindles dropped three catches, excusing himself: 'Oh, sir! I don't know what came over me, sir.'

George replied generously: 'Well, we've never known you drop a full glass in the club, Brindles.'

Toby held two brilliant ones, making Aubrey complain: 'Thought you said you were a cricket duffer? Spent your time at Eton messing about in boats.'

'But at prep school I was frightfully good,' Toby explained blandly. 'I wonder if I've any other buried talents needing unearthing?' he asked Miss Frobisher at second slip.

The Gallant Winco reported that his hip was going, and his wound from a Messerschmitt cannon-shell starting to gyp. He left the pitch, substituted by an opponent who under the gentlemanly unwritten rules of cricket was to field as zealously as the others, unless presented with a serious chance of getting anyone out.

Harker-Hewitt bowled three overs of fast hostility, and approached George clutching his chest.

'You knew I'd a weak heart, didn't you?'

'You poor fellow! I'd no idea,' George sympathized.

'Can't possibly face another over. Sorry. Must go and lie down. Otherwise . . .'

'Of course,' George said anxiously. 'Do you want a doctor? The Professor's son's at square leg.'

Harker-Hewitt shook his head silently and staggered off.

Six overs later, George dispatched the young doctor to see how the casualties were surviving.

'They're in the tent,' he reported cheerfully. 'Already into their second bottle of champagne.'

George groaned. '*England, Their England*! Like the redoubtable Major Hawker, who terrified seven batsmen clean bowled six of them, and broke a stump, then got stuck in the pub all afternoon. Now he won't bowl anything more fearsome than donkey-drops for the rest of the innings.'

Lunch.

'Can't we give you something to eat?' Stephen invited liberally.

The club team had gathered on a hump of long grass with their picnic.

'A lobster, perhaps?' he suggested. 'Some quail in aspic? We've loads.'

'Thank you, we've brought our rations,' George told him stiffly.

'The English countryman,' muttered Aubrey, staring into the lively chattering marquee.

George forked a pickled onion from the large bottle to enhance his bread and cheese. He said disgustedly: 'That lot couldn't tell a cowpat from a *crêpe Suzette*.'

'Townspeople suffer painful fantasies about the country,' Aubrey decided. 'All those glossies they read about life in the shires. They're the rustic equivalent of *Playboy* and *Penthouse*.'

'We've friends in Town always talking about "moving out",' Gloria remarked.

'To be among *real* people, you know, with *real* whole-food to eat, *real* air to breathe and *real* wildlife twittering on the thatch.'

'Where they could feel the significance of life and watch the harvest festivals come round,' Aubrey added.

'Ending up a mouldering heap, I suppose, beneath those rugged elms, that yew-tree's shade?' George quoted disgruntledly.

'One couple moved into "The Old Forge", installed a farmhouse kitchen chosen from the Sunday supplements, a giant bellows from a Chelsea antique shop, and front door coachlamps from Harrods,' Aubrey recalled.

'I believe she cooked in green wellies,' said Gloria.

Aubrey shortly gathered the beer cans and went seeking the pavilion litter-basket.

George said to her: 'I still think of an English village as G. K. Chesterton did – a miraculous relic, like the relic of a great saint.'

She smiled tenderly. 'George, you're an incurable romantic.'

'You told me once that I wasn't romantic enough. Remember? When we were in Cannes. When Aubrey was in New York.'

She said in alarm: 'I hope to God you never mention that in the club?'

'That would definitely not be cricket.'

Gloria smiled again. 'I don't know if it amazes or amuses me, that you could make love for a solid fortnight to a fellow-clubman's wife.'

'Nothing in the rules against it.'

'Aubrey says it's the unwritten ones which matter.'

'There's only two. Don't be a bore. And put up with the members who are.'

'Surely, what you get up to outside the club must produce *some* effect inside it?' she said impatiently.

'Not really. We never much bother what happens out of each other's sight. If marriage operated on the same system, it would be a much happier affair.'

'Did Vanessa go off with a member?'

'Good Lord, no. She couldn't stand any of them.'

'She was very fond of Aubrey.'

'*Was* she!'

'What do you make of your sexy new secretary?'

'Members would not be expected to become over-familiar with the staff,' George told her loftily.

'Aubrey fancies her.'

'*Does* he!'

It was time for the resumption of play.

6

The club won!

Credit must be given the Professor's son, who scored one hundred and fifty-two not out, the rest contributing fifteen.

Our star batsman suffered as much difficulty finding someone to stay with him as a club bore in the bar.

Miss Frobisher doughtily stonewalled until bowled by Stephen, who looked as self-satisfied as St George who had slain the lady as well as the dragon.

Harker-Hewitt elevated himself to a club hero by steadfastly blocking one end, while young Tom dispatched the bowlers like a naval salvo into the horse-pond.

The winning run was hit as the landlord shot back the opening-time bolts of the Red Cow.

'I shall leave your cheque for £500 with the club porter on Monday morning,' said Stephen painfully, the batsmen reaching the pavilion to vigorous applause.

Harker-Hewitt smiled. 'How kind.'

Stephen shortly reappeared among the celebratory team in the saloon bar. He looked as though he had discovered nobbling among the jury.

'I brought along the latest list of members in my cricket-bag.'

He flourished the claret-coloured crested booklet.

'I regret to say, I find no trace of your son's membership,' he accused the Professor.

'How odd. Must have been elected since it was printed.'

'With great respect, I disagree. I should have remembered your son among the new members. I always look at the notice board, to see who's dead,' Stephen told him crossly.

'We can elect him under rule number whatsitsname.'

The Gallant Winco looked pleased with himself. 'Giving great service to the club. That's what I call making a century for us.'

'The century was nevertheless made when he was *not* a member of the club,' Stephen objected coldly.

'You lawyers are so legalistic,' George complained irritably.

'There's another rule, Wing Commander–'

Miss Frobisher, still in her Wimbledon dress, stood bright-eyed among them.

'In an emergency, the secretary and a senior member of the committee – like Mr Gifford – can make decisions for the club with retrospective effect. It was passed in wartime.'

'When the club risked demolition overnight in the Blitz?' the Gallant Winco recalled with relish. 'Or was it by the Zeps?'

'I think it was when the committee was concerned at the delay in relieving Ladysmith, Wing Commander.'

'Suppose we should start repealing some of those old rules,' the Gallant Winco commented. 'Not much call for a free nosebag for your horses these days.'

'You knew he was a cricket blue, and not a member, when you made that bet.' Stephen eyed Harker-Hewitt as if demanding the death penalty, embellished by drawing and quartering.

'Of course,' Harker-Hewitt told him easily. 'Because I was confident a sportsman wouldn't quibble about such things. I anyway intended giving it to the club fund which handles Brindles' old age.'

'I think this is a matter for the committee,' threatened Stephen.

'So when young Tom here is eventually put up for membership,' Aubrey said angrily, 'which is the dear Professor's most cherished ambition, he'll be blackballed as a matter of course.'

Stephen paused. 'I hadn't thought of that.'

'Really, Stephen!' George complained. 'What's £500 to you? We saved that by bringing our own lunch.'

Stephen stroked his jowls. 'Possibly I'm being a little churlish.'

'You're being a pain in the arse,' Aubrey made the ungentlemanly expression.

'I'm sorry,' Stephen said, suddenly pathetic. 'It's the disappointment, I suppose. I thought we were going to beat the living daylights out of you.'

He looked more cheerful. 'Let's forget our disagreement. It's always a relief when a grievance can be extinguished by the exercise of one's own good nature.'

'Have a drink,' Harker-Hewitt invited. 'Or are you engaged with your friends?'

'They are folding their tent, like the Arabs, and as silently stealing away,' Stephen said sadly. 'Country people have a lot of parties on Saturday evenings.'

They had several drinks.

Stephen began telling Miss Frobisher how adorable she was at cricket.

George sang the champagne chorus from *Die Fledermaus* in German and Carmen's *Habanera* in French.

Aubrey started reciting Gray's *Elegy in a Country Churchyard*, but forgot it after the beetle wheeling his droning flight.

Miss Frobisher said she must go and change.

Ten minutes later, Stephen came through the front door of the Red Cow, holding a closed right eye.

'Went out for a Jimmy Riddle,' he explained hastily. 'Stupidly bumped into the door of the gents.'

Five minutes later, Miss Frobisher came through the front door of the Red Cow, looking furious.

'Quentin! We're going home.'

Harker-Hewitt put his arm round Miss Frobisher.

'Tried to rape you, did he, darling?'

'Yes. I hit him with a stump.'

'But it was all a dreadful mistake,' lamented Stephen loudly.

'Shall I have a look at that eye?' volunteered Tom. 'It'll be as black as a Christmas pudding in the morning.'

'I was only offering a friendly kiss,' Stephen explained desperately. 'To thank her for organizing your team.'

'This had better not get round the club,' said George sternly.

'No more than the bet on the match,' added Aubrey.

'There's a Rolls just drawn up,' observed Gloria from the window.

'My wife come to fetch me,' mumbled Stephen. 'Please say I was struck by a bouncer.'

'Forget it, darling.' Harket-Hewitt kissed Miss Frobisher. 'We'll go out to dinner, and an early bed.'

'You know Miss Frobisher well?' George suggested mildly.

'We live together, Mr Gifford,' she imparted. 'It's so convenient for the club, two stops on the tube to St James's.'

'Now it's hands off Miss Frobisher, I suppose?' observed Aubrey to George as they climbed into the 'minibus'.

'It's always a relief when a sexual urge can be extinguished by the exercise of one's own good nature.'

'Thanks, dad!' Tom laughed as he reached his car. 'It's been the funniest day for years.'

'We old folk still manage to amuse ourselves,' the Professor told him wistfully.

'Dad – can I ask you a favour? Put me up for the club.'

The Professor stared into his son's eyes. Silently he clasped his hand.

Tom grinned.

'Don't blub, dad. Stiff upper lip.'

FIVE

1

Monday was Irish stew day.

At my usual perch upon the bum-warmer in the morning room, taking my pre-lunch pinkers beside the 'smokeless' coal fire on a chilly autumn morning, my heart plummeted.

George had observed from his favourite chair beside Lord Curzon: 'There's a fascinating story in *The Notebooks of a Spinster Lady* by Lady Caroline Holland, a lady-in-waiting to Queen Victoria–'

Aubrey groaned from his own favourite chair: 'George, we all know that story.'

George pointed out briskly: 'We have three new members with us. I'm sure they'd be most interested to hear it.'

Aubrey rose with his pinkers. 'I'm going to the bar.'

George was one of the club's seasoned raconteurs.

Nothing is more infuriating to lose than an opportunity.

The shaft of wit unloosed, rattling in the quiver when leaving for home is a frustratingly useless social weapon.

It once provoked the disdainful phrase: *l'esprit de l'escalier*, Gallic wit being as great an item of local pride as the cooking.

Talkative members of the Albany Club therefore composed their elegant spontaneous remarks in the hall going in, though this necessitated experience in manoeuvering the conversation to let them off.

Many other members – particularly in the artistic occupations of literature, newspapers and advertising – polished their phrases like their shoes before leaving home.

George in addition required a quorum, so as not to waste *bons mots.*

This was now provided by the three new members, so overawed they would have smilingly listened to him reciting *Beowulf* all the way through.

Other gentlemen present were Toby the MP, engrossed in the *New Statesman,* and Herbert who never objected to anything.

'It was Lady Holland who bestowed us the phrase "We are not amused",' George started as usual. 'An unfortunate equerry at Windsor had ventured during dinner on some anecdote with the spice of impropriety. It happened in 1899.'

The new boys remained respectfully agog.

'Lady Caroline tells the delightful tale of a colonel arriving at his club – not the In and Out, which takes only officers, though possibly the Garrick, which takes absolutely anyone,' he continued predictably, sipping his pinkers.

'This colonel was handed by the porter an envelope with a turned-in flap, in which he was surprised to find a tailor's bill, accompanied by a letter "reproachful, urgent, even menacing".'

George explained: 'It was addressed to an actor, of the same name. The colonel naturally handed it back, and made for the smoking room. Minutes later, the actor appeared holding the same envelope. Taking a prominent position before the fire, elbow on mantelpiece, he read the letter – now elevating his eyebrows, now with a smothered exclamation, now with an expressive shrug. Having thus attracted an audience, the actor drew himself up, and slowly crumpling the letter with long, delicate fingers, dropped it gently into the fire, then turned away with the pitying remark: "Poor little woman!"'

Toby tossed aside the *New Statesman.* 'God, you haven't been telling that story again?'

'Well, I think it very charming.'

'I thought *Cinderella* was very charming the first time I heard it, which seems equally long ago.'

George ignored this.

'I'm trying to interest my publishers in an anthology of club stories, as a matter of fact. Surely you know the one about Lord Birkenhead at the Athenaeum–'

But George's audience, like the Boojum's, had softly and suddenly vanished away.

He sipped his pinkers, consoled that the gentlemen now arriving for lunch must include at least one eager to know all about Lord Birkenhead and the Athenaeum.

At the front door, Hawkins was gravely informing Miss Frobisher: 'Sir Isaac Newton's been giving more trouble, madam.'

'Oh, dear!'

Hawkins turned the chunk of stonework in his fingers.

'His right ear, fell into Pall Mall this morning. Remember Sir Isaac's nose? Nearly flattened a policeman. And Oliver Cromwell almost killed a gentleman going for lunch at the Traveller's Club.'

'I'm afraid those busts outside the library windows are simply disintegrating, like other bits of historical London,' Miss Frobisher decided sadly.

'The whole façade, madam, if I may say so, is unworthy of a gentlemen's club,' Hawkins told her frankly.' 'It's so dirty, it resembles a railway terminus when the trains used to go chuff-chuff.'

'I know, Hawkins, but it would cost the earth to renovate. The committee's already discussed the matter. The club simply can't afford it.'

'Perhaps Mr Willi Smith might help, madam? You always see his name up there on cranes, building things.'

Miss Frobisher was doubtful. 'Mr Smith has already been very generous towards the club. Though I suppose I can raise it again at the next committee.'

'What shall I do with it?' Hawkins offered her the ear.

'Put it with the other members' lost property, I suppose. Good morning, sir!'

Miss Frobisher smiled, as Orlando entered the club with customary flourish.

'A very good morning to you, Miss Frobisher. And to you, Hawkins. A nip in the air, don't you think? The mists and mellow fruitfulness will soon have us by the scruff of our necks.'

He advanced into the morning room.

'Brindles! My usual. The Buck's fizz at the Albany is quite the best in London – except at Buck's Club, naturally,' he proclaimed to George and myself.

'It's the dollop of Cointreau which does it,' George agreed sagely.

Orlando was cherished in the club, like Brindles, or Lord Rosebery's vanished horse's hoof.

He was an actor, a vivid buttonhole in the sober tailoring of our membership.

A lithe, slender gentleman, his putty-coloured face moulded itself into myriad expressions, his hands gestured as delicately as swooping swallows, his talk bounced as playfully as a child's balloon, his dyed hair was paid the supreme club compliment of disregard.

The club had elected earlier Thespians – Henry Irving, after he was shockingly blackballed at the Garrick, doubtless through jealousy, though he was known to be rather noisy.

Our other mummers were generally knighted first, a reasonable guarantee of predictable behaviour, though they tended in the club to overact the role of gentleman.

'What are you in at the moment, Orlando?' I enquired politely. 'I might even run to a couple of stalls. Haven't had a night on the town for ages.'

'Dear Boy! How kind. I've rather turned against the West End for a bit,' he explained. 'Ghastly lot of plays on these days. So many revivals, strolling down Shaftesbury Avenue's like playing the gravediggers' scene in

Hamlet. I think I was in most of them when they first opened.'

'Saw one of your old movies, Orlando,' mentioned George. 'Had to stay in last Sunday afternoon.'

'Ah! With dear Kenny More and delicious Kay Kendal!' Orlando chuckled.

'Must have been made about forty years ago,' I calculated.

'Something like that,' he said briefly. 'Do you know, the biggest shock to the drama, since miracle plays shifted from the church to the marketplace in the thirteenth century, is old movies on TV. Oh, thank you, Brindles. The performances of Garrick, Keen, Beerbohm Tree, are melted into air, into thin air.'

He gestured gracefully with his champagne glass.

'But lovely Ralph Richardson, brilliant Peter Sellers, will dazzle and glitter into eternity.'

'You know the story about Lord Birkenhead, the Lord Chancellor?' intruded George. 'Every day on his way home from the House of Lords he dropped into the Athenaeum Club for a pee, even though he wasn't a member.'

'Yes, and when the Athenaeum got their porter to complain, Lord Birkenhead said: "Oh, it's a club, too, is it?"' Orlando told him shortly.

Brindles struck the gong.

When the month proffered an 'r', Orlando lunched off a dozen Whitstables and a half-bottle of 'The Widow'. How we envied the style in which 'stars of stage and screen' lived!

'A meal fit for a king!' he declared, the first succulent bivalve slipping down anointed with a squeeze of lemon, chilli vinegar and dash of Tabasco.

'When I first saw you, Orlando, you were a king,' Willi said admiringly across the long coffee-room table. 'King Richard III.'

'Now is the winter of our discontent Made glorious

summer by this sun of York, yes it's a lovely part, though the hunchback's a bit of a bore.'

'I'd just arrived in England. I was but a boy. I had no money,' Willi made the unexpected revelation. 'I sat up there in the gods. Your wonderful performance made me realize what England is all about.'

'As Richard III is full of scheming, treachery, murder and sex, old boy, I suppose you're right,' observed George.

'It was at the Old Vic,' Willi ruminated.

'Charming little theatre,' Orlando conceded, gesticulating with his oyster-shell. 'If utterly impossible to get to, over the river.'

'I love the theatre, but it does so ruin an evening,' Aubrey grumbled. 'Dine first, you go to sleep. Dine after, your tummy-rumbles disturb the stalls right through the last act.'

Willi continued solemnly: 'By the time at the end when you needed a horse, I wept.'

'"A horse! A horse! My kingdom for a horse", how kind, dear boy.'

'I have never forgotten it.'

'How *very kind*.'

After the treacle sponge and custard, the ground rice with raspberry jam and Aubrey's prunes, for a bit of fun we all strolled out to the notice board to see who was dead.

'Mr Smith–'

Miss Frobisher approached Orlando.

'This is rather embarrassing, but I've discovered that the secretary has somehow overlooked sending out bar bills to a large number of members. They go back quite a long way,' she apologized. 'Some to the Victory celebrations at the end of the War. I'm afraid yours is rather large, sir.'

'I'll settle it now,' said Orlando cheerfully, feeling in his jacket. 'Oh, damn! Haven't my chequebook. Next time I'm in the club.'

'Of course, sir.'

'Glass of port?' Aubrey offered.

'Dear boy, must dash. Just remembered, have to look into Fortnum's for some caviar, some people coming in tonight. Hawkins! Call me a taxi.'

'Certainly, sir.'

'Oh, it's started to rain,' Orlando noticed. He added considerately: 'Don't you bother, it'll take hours, I'll get one myself.'

He turned back from the front door, inspected the iron stand loaded with members' umbrellas, selected one and left.

He hurried round the corner of Pall Mall, glanced behind him, joined the queue in a bus shelter and boarded the next bus, flashing his OAP's pass.

2

The following steak and kidney pie day (Wednesday), Miss Frobisher took the committee meeting in the library.

The Gallant Winco told her she needed the experience, but we all knew he was only a lazy sod.

Nobody was blackballed.

'The last candidate was a close-run thing,' Lord Cotswold imparted quietly to Miss Frobisher, returning from the ballot boxes to the long library table. 'A very decent Labour MP. Toby Jeavons, our Tory MP, tried getting up a gang to blackball him.'

Miss Frobisher looked shocked.

'Oh, there's a good deal of bullying goes on behind the bike-shed,' he informed her casually. 'Next business?'

'A member resigning from the club, Lord Cotswold. Mr Tankerton.'

'Old Tankers!' murmured everyone.

'His letter is sadly short.' She read: 'I regret I am shortly to be declared bankrupt, and resign from the Albany Club to spare myself the ignomy of being expelled'.

Gloomy silence blanketed the table.

'Well known in the City,' Aubrey contributed helpfully. 'Came unstuck in cocoa futures.'

Lord Cotswold reached for the claret-coloured Rule Book.

'I think we know well enough the rules say that any bankrupt shall cease to be a member of the club *ipso facto*. Would it be gentlemanly to accept his resignation?'

Melancholy nods consented.

'Send him the necessary letter, Miss Frobisher. And the club's sympathy. Next item?'

'A member has written, complaining: "In the past twelve months I have had five umbrellas taken – entirely by mistake, on every occasion, I am sure – from the stand outside the porter's lodge, despite their being engraved with my initials, and latterly my full name. Will the committee consider taking drastic action against such inconsiderate and immoral members?"'

'If a member brings his umbrella to the club on a wet day, it's a risk he must take,' Lord Cotswold said forthrightly. 'Members regard umbrellas as communal property.'

'Like library books,' added Aubrey.

'I'd be dreadfully worried if mine weren't pinched from the club library,' sighed George. 'I'd be losing my popularity.'

'No action,' said Lord Cotswold curtly. 'The club's annual dinner–'

'Oh! The secretary regrets he'll be on leave–' remembered Miss Frobisher.

'You'll take his place.'

'But I'm a woman!'

'So's the Queen. Agreed?'

'Agreed!' roared the committee.

'Thank . . . thank you, gentlemen.'

Miss Frobisher looked in danger of a good blub again.

'The committee needs as usual to select a member as a guest of honour,' Lord Cotswold continued briskly. 'I propose Willi Smith.'

Silence.

'Willi has been very good to us.'

Silence.

'He paid for the modernization of the kitchen, when it was shut by the drains people as insanitary. We hope he will now pay for the refurbishment of the club frontage, which is falling into Pall Mall like the walls of Jericho.'

Silence.

Aubrey coughed. 'But Willi is hardly a . . . this *is* a club for gentlemen.'

'Come off it, Aubrey,' George corrected him. 'It's a club for people like you and me.'

'Agreed?' persisted Lord Cotswold. 'Good! Miss Frobisher, dispatch the requisite letter. Any other business? I declare the meeting closed. I expect the bar's open.'

3

Orlando boiled his breakfast-egg in the saucepan of water for his tea.

A diversion for gentlemen among other gentlemen in clubs is: 'Speculating on what is going on within those tents and curtains of their souls, their coats and waistcoats.'

As William Makepeace Thackeray said this, they were our souls and our waistcoats.

Clubs offer the charming innecessity of knowing fellow members intimately.

No one at the Albany bothered where Herbert lived, or Orlando lived. We knew where Willi lived, but only because it got into the newspapers.

A knock came on Orlando's door.

'Do come in!'

Mrs Bartlett was youngish and fairish, neat in her pinny. She held some letters.

'Good morning, Mrs Bartlett!' Orlando greeted her warmly. 'May I offer you a cup of tea?'

'No, thank you, Mr Smith. I only brought up your post.'

'How very kind.'

Mrs Bartlett hesitated at the door of the little room with unmade bed, washbasin, cracked ceiling and view of chimney-stacks and TV aerials, crammed with framed signed photographs of Orlando with extinguished stars like Noël Coward, Marilyn Monroe and George Bernard Shaw.

Orlando in brocade dressing-gown poured boiling water from the ring by the gas fire into a delicate china teapot.

'Mr Smith, you've had one of my rooms now for two years. Though I couldn't wish for a nicer tenant–'

'How very kind.'

Orlando deftly cupped the egg.

'But the rent for this bed-sitter is three-and-a-half months overdue.'

'Nobody could be more sorry than myself,' Orlando confessed.

'I'm sure.'

'The stage is utterly heartless,' he explained apologetically. 'As Samuel Johnson remarked: "We that live to please, must please to live." I stopped being pleasing.'

'I know things are difficult–'

'Dear, dear, Dinah!' Orlando reached for the silver-framed photograph of a dreamy blonde. 'When my dear wife died two years ago I was heartbroken, Mrs Bartlett. Utterly heartbroken. But the poor dear was so dreadfully extravagant. Left me enormous debts. Astronomical! And I was already out of work. Without my debts, I might possibly manage. I draw the Queen's pension. Do you know, somebody recognized me the other day in the post office? I had to pretend I was buying a stamp.'

'I don't want to press you, Mr Smith,' said Mrs Bartlett uneasily, affected by the performance. 'But these rooms are my livelihood–'

'We met when I was on tour,' Orlando continued tenderly to the photograph. 'In dear Terry Rattigan's *French Without Tears*. That lovely line! "What is the French for she has ideas above her station? *Elle a des idées au-dessus de sa gare*".'

This was lost on the audience.

'Mr Smith, if you don't pay your arrears by the end of the month, you'll have to go,' said Mrs Bartlett firmly.

'Indeed, Mrs Bartlett, indeed,' Orlando agreed readily. 'Luckily, I have many friends. I'm sure one of them will be most pleased to take me in.'

'I'm glad to hear it, Mr Smith. I'd feel awful, making you homeless.'

'Though of course, I shall settle my debts as a matter of honour.'

'I'm sure, Mr Smith.' There was silence. 'Well, good morning, Mr Smith.'

'Good morning, Mrs Bartlett.'

Orlando gloomily cracked his egg.

He dressed, and went for a walk.

He shivered at the sign: 'Salvation Army Hostel For Homeless', in the ugly, litter-strewn, graffiti-emblazoned street outside.

A down-and-out surrounded with empty bottles sat on the pavement. Orlando felt in his pocket for a coin, but decided against it.

He saw a telephone box.

He had an idea.

4

Orlando arrived at the club shortly before one o'clock.

'I've a luncheon guest, at rather short notice,' he announced to Hawkins.

'I'll let you know when he arrives, sir. Good morning, sir,' Hawkins added, as Willi followed Orlando through the front door. 'Your letters, sir.'

'Wonderful! shouted Willi, in the middle of the chessboard-floored hall.

Gentlemen stared.

'I have been paid a magnificent compliment! I am guest of honour at the club's annual dinner!'

'I *know*, Mr Smith,' smiled Miss Frobisher, approaching. 'I signed the letter.'

Willi was almost blubbing.

'This is the greatest thing in my life. I am like a cat with two tails. I promise I shall make a very short speech, and only one joke. And I shall get some caviar and grouse for everybody, from the hotel I own in Park Lane.'

He wandered into the morning room, stupefied.

'Mr Shelley's forehead, madam.' Hawkins confronted Miss Frobisher. 'Came down at breakfast-time.'

'Oh, dear!'

George and Aubrey pushed through the front door with Toby the MP.

All three made for Mr Gladstone.

'Our club chairman must be out of his noble mind,' murmured Toby, at the gorgeous urinals.

'Making Willi guest of honour at the dinner? He's been very generous to the Albany, old man,' Aubrey reminded him.

Toby shrugged. 'You can buy yourself a peerage – if the money's good enough. But I do not agree with the purchase of honours in a gentleman's club.'

'Who else would you stand a free dinner, then?' George asked pointedly, as they crossed to the wash-basins and Imperial Leather.

'We've a former Minister of Education. There's Osbert, a distinguished civil servant.'

'All quite as dull as *The Times*' leaders,' George dismissed them. 'My dear Toby, Willi brings to the club the exotic colour of the zigane, the czardas, the goulash.'

Toby dried his hands on the huckaback.

'It's bad enough now being part of Europe. We don't want a lot of ruddy Europeans throwing their weight about over here.'

'Can't do much about the dinner at this stage,' Aubrey said decisively, picking up a communal comb.

'We can,' Toby told him crisply. 'I'm getting a lobby up, to have the invitation withdrawn. As an MP, I'm rather good at that sort of thing.'

George made the gentlemanly objection: 'Bit hard on Willi, isn't it?'

'Oh, I'm sure he'll blub into his Krugerrands. You two chaps are senior members. Will you join me?'

Aubrey inspected himself in the gilt-edged mirror.

'Matter of fact, I think I will,' he decided. 'Willi *is* rather awful.'

'I regard the choice as an insult to the club,' Toby said fiercely. 'George?'

'As you MPs say, I shall reserve my position.'

'As us MPs say, sitting on the fence,' grinned Toby.

As they reappeared behind Mr Gladstone, Hawkins was announcing to Orlando: 'Your guest, sir.'

'How wonderful to see you again!' declared a fat, pink, bald, tweedy gentleman.

'Walter! How good of you to drop absolutely everything and come.'

They embraced.

'I'd always put off anything to meet you, Orlando.' Walter grinned broadly. 'Ever since Margaret Lockwood was a Wicked Lady.'

They sat in the coffee room at one of the small guest tables beyond the long one, between full-length portraits of Carlyle and Darwin darkened by a century of oily emanations from the club menus.

'Good morning, sir!' Rosie our 'nippy' greeted Orlando. 'Oh – excuse me.'

She changed round the two club menus.

Walter smiled. 'How gentlemanly! The prices are on the host's menu, but not on the guest's.'

'The tomato soup is very good,' suggested Orlando.

'I think I'll have a plate of smoked salmon.'

'And a tomato soup,' Orlando ordered for himself. 'The shepherd's pie is a great favourite,' he recommended.

'I'll have a grouse,' decided Walter.

'How would you like it, sir?' Rosie scribbled on her pad.

'Pinkish.'

'It's served with game chips and breadcrumbs, sir, on *foie gras* toast.'

'Ah,' said Walter.

'Shepherd's pie,' Orlando ordered gloomily. 'And a decanter of the club claret.'

'Thank you, sir.'

'There's an old movie you produced, Walter, with me and dear Dinah, on television tonight,' said Orlando, vaguely getting down to business.

'Rather *late* tonight,' Walter had to admit.

'Pity we don't get paid for it.'

'When I produced that film, I don't think television had been invented,' Walter said cheerfully. 'Or it consisted only of Gilbert Harding.'

'Then we had a British film industry,' sighed Orlando.

'A very good industry.'

'A cottage industry,' Orlando ruminated. 'With lovingly handmade products, like our Harris tweed and clotted cream.'

'Movie-making was so easy then. I drove the Rolls to the City, raised a few thousand quid, went out to Pinewood and shot it. Now, of course, you can't even park in the City.'

Rosie brought the club claret.

'Can't tell you how impressed I am, Orlando, being in your club,' Walter said appreciatively. 'Those lovely paintings! This wonderful woodwork.' He unfurled his napkin. 'Starched linen! It's all priceless.'

'Hello, Orlando!'

Willi was passing their table.

'You have a film on my TV channel tonight. I shall stay up specially to watch.'

'Who's that?' Walter's interested glance followed him to the long table.

'Willi Smith. You know, the multi-multi-multi-millionaire. But here he's just an ordinary member of the club,' Orlando said proudly.

'The possession of large amounts of money is not, as some people think, a virtue,' Walter philosophized.

'Nor, as some other people think, is the possession of none. Walter, dear boy, this is rather embarrassing, but could you make me a small loan? Only the odd thousand. To tide me over.'

Walter was deeply shocked.

'You want to borrow money from me?'

'I'm afraid I'm reduced to that,' Orlando said miserably. 'It's very sad.'

'But Orlando! I haven't produced a movie since Joan Collins was a prefect in the Rank Charm School. I grabbed the chance of a meeting today, because I was hoping to borrow money from *you*.'

Rosie served them.

'Enjoy your lunch,' murmured Orlando.

5

That night Orlando visited the agent who had ten per cent of his life's earnings, but he apologized that times were hard.

As he raised the latchkey to his own front door, a big man in a lumberjacket separated from the darkness.

'Orlando Smith?' He grabbed the lapels of Orlando's vicuna overcoat.

'Take your hands off me!' cried Orlando in terror.

The man paid no notice.

'Hiding down here, are you? But we found you.'

'Who *are* you?'

'Remember Mr Garfunkle?'

'Garfunkle? Garfunkle?' Orlando searched his acquaintances.

'Of Hatton Garden.'

'Oh, *that* Mr Garfunkle! And how is dear Mr Garfunkle?'

'He's very well. I'm a friend of his. That diamond necklace you bought five years ago. It's not fully paid for.'

Orlando was surprised. 'Really?'

'I'd like it back.' The man gripped tighter.

'Impossible.'

'Why?'

'I popped it,' Orlando explained simply.

'I want the money.'

'I'm sure you do.'

'Plus interest. I'll spare you the index-linked.'

The man released him.

'I'll see what I can do,' Orlando promised breathlessly.

'Otherwise I'll be back. With another friend.' He hit Orlando in the stomach.

Poor Orlando!

He staggered into the house, climbed upstairs by the bannisters, tottered gasping into his little room, soaked towel under cold tap and wrapped it round his head, collapsed into creaky chair.

He remembered the television.

He hastily switched on the set beside the gas-ring, and there he was, young, debonair, handsome and in black and white.

He was driving an open Bentley down a country lane, beside him the dear departed Dinah.

Orlando covered his face with his hands and had a little blub.

'You own a lovely car,' said Dinah.

'About the only thing I do own,' he told her.

They kissed at the wheel.

Orlando removed his hands from his face. This was the bit when he ran over the Duke.

'Frightfully sorry, sir,' he apologized, picking up A. E. Matthews.

'Do you know who I am, you young puppy? And that, if I am not mistaken, is my daughter.'

'How terribly convenient. I'd just called to ask to marry her.'

'What!'

Orlando in his bedsitter started laughing.

'I observed you had a slight accident, your Grace, and brought a restorative,' offered Alastair Sim, the film butler with silver salver.

Tweed-jacketed young Orlando snapped to attention and barked: 'Sir!'

'What *is* going on?' wondered Dinah, while the Duke gulped whisky and soda.

The Orlando we love at the Albany laughed heartily. The butler was his old colonel in the army, desperate for a job.

'We seem in for an interesting weekend,' Dinah observed charmingly.

The plot crankily unwound. Orlando slapped his thighs, threw back his head and roared.

How priceless a gift, to laugh at yourself.

6

Willi entered the morning room, ashen-faced.

It was Friday (kipper day).

George looked up from the *Listener*, startled.

'George, I must talk to you.'

Willi glanced at Herbert, who was behind *The Times*.

'Outside.'

He waved his handful of letters towards Mr Gladstone.

The members' bog was empty.

The stout glass tank above the magnificent marble-girt

urinals abruptly loosened its Niagara down the morning's yet unsullied porcelain. A member had once stocked it with goldfish, which were regularly left flapping and gasping on its empty floor, and was asked to resign.

'Something terrible has happened.'

Willi handed George a letter, which read:

Dear Mr Smith,

As attempts to obtain a reply from your home address have repeatedly failed, we are obliged to seek you at your club. Unless our clients' accounts are settled by next Monday, we shall file a Petition of Bankruptcy against you.

Yours sincerely,

Gentle Persuasion Debt Collectors Ltd

'It *is* terrible, Willi!' George agreed readily. 'When you go bankrupt, the City of London will quiver, governments topple, widows and orphans starve worldwide and stockbrokers drop into Wall Street like a ticker-tape welcome.'

'No, no! The thumbscrews aren't on me,' Willi corrected him impatiently. 'It's addressed to Orlando Smith. I opened another gentleman's letter. What a terrible thing to do in the club!'

George consoled him: 'An honest mistake.'

Willi reflected uneasily: 'Perhaps I shouldn't have changed my name. It could have waited till my peerage.'

'Poor Orlando!' George exclaimed sympathetically. 'He'll have to leave the club.'

Willi nodded glumly. '*Ipso facto*.'

George wondered: 'How'd he get in such a mess? Backing plays, I suppose. I've seen chaps in frightful financial trouble just because they fancied some actress. You'd best keep pretty quiet, and give it back to the porter,' he advised. 'Hawkins keeps some sticky tape stuff, for members getting infuriated at something they read in the newspapers.'

Willi rejoined George in the morning room from the porter's lodge.

They ordered pinkers and champers.

Orlando shortly strolled in, envelope sticking from pocket of snugly-waisted brown tweed jacket.

'Morning, chaps! Lovely day, if chilly for the time of year.'

He warmed his hands before the 'smokeless' fire.

'Brindles! Buck's fizz, please.'

'Very good, sir.'

'Don't open it,' said Willi, with unwonted bashfulness.

Orlando was puzzled.

'Chuck it in the fire,' Willi advised gravely.

'What? Oh, this letter! Only be a circular. I tell people never to write me here. Hawkins keeps them for months, until you look at a loose end.'

'Come outside,' Willi commanded.

Orlando arched an eyebrow. Carrying his Buck's fizz, he followed the pair past Mr Gladstone.

'I opened your letter in error,' Willi confessed solemnly, waiting for the hissing cascade down the urinals to gurgle away. 'Frightfully sorry, old chap.'

Orlando arched both eyebrows.

'I'd better read it then, I suppose?'

He gave a tragic sigh.

'Oh, dear. Well, I tried spinning out the last act as long as possible.'

He smiled wryly. 'You look flatteringly disbelieving, George, dear boy. But I'm skint. The curtain rang down on my career years ago. Nobody in the club noticed, of course. Acting isn't thought by gentlemen a serious occupation.'

Orlando's jauntiness peeled from him like the brilliant shell of the plovers' eggs he so enjoyed every May.

'I shall miss the club frightfully. Since I moved to the little place in Clapham – since the dear old gel died – the only touch of my old grandeur was coming here whenever I dared to afford it.'

He raised his Buck's fizz.

'Farewell, dear old club! "Farewell! A long farewell, to all my greatness! This is the state of man: today he puts forth the tender leaves of hope; tomorrow blossoms, And bears his blushing honours thick upon him; The third day comes a frost, a killing frost." I shall, of course, settle my bar bill first.'

'Hold your hounds,' Willi commanded gruffly. 'You are not resigning from the club.'

Orlando began protesting: '*Ipso facto*–'

'I shall give a bank guarantee for all your debts.'

'Which I shall utterly refuse to accept,' Orlando told him immediately.

Willi fixed him with an eye before which finance ministers flinched, and bankers looked nervously towards their window-ledges.

'You will accept it, please. I have not forgotten Richard III. I have been seeking means to repay the inspiration of your performance ever since.'

Orlando looked at George helplessly.

'My dear fellow,' George said. 'Let us celebrate our vast pleasure at retaining you in our shabby nest with a bottle of the Jubilee champagne.'

Willi took Orlando's sleeve.

'There is one condition. No one but we three shall ever know about it in the club. Ever.'

'Cross my heart,' agreed Orlando willingly.

He smilingly upended his Buck's fizz, as the cleansing torrent descended again.

'Made up your mind?' Toby asked George in the morning room.

'Yes, old boy. Go ahead with your little scheme to do

Willi out of a dinner. I shall report your ungentlemanly behaviour towards a fellow member to the committee. Also your canvassing to blackball that Labour MP, which is against club rules. Can I get you a drink?'

The Club dinner was the best since Churchill came.

We ate Willi's caviar and grouse, followed by the club chef's famous if tasteless syllabub and leathery welsh rarebit. Brindles served the Coronation claret, which the committee wanted to get rid of as it was going off.

Willi told his joke, which being about a silly foreigner drew roars and applause.

'A gentlemen's club is sadly misunderstood,' Lord Cotswold ended before the dinner-jacketed members. 'People think we are privileged, prejudiced, prehistoric. But the essence of a club is friendship. Nothing wrong with that? We see each other growing sometimes richer, perhaps poorer–'

Orlando between George and Aubrey smiled faintly.

'Often fatter, always older. We die, but we are remembered. Sometimes more fondly than when we are still alive. We are a band of brothers. Unique in this age – a band of brothers with no axe to grind.'

Slaps to the shining mahogany tabletops.

'Lady–'

He smiled fondly at Miss Frobisher, delightfully *décolleté* beside him.

'And gentlemen – the club!'

We leapt up.

'The club!' we shouted.

It was enough to make a chap blub into his port.

SIX

1

Aubrey left the Albany Club, briefcase in hand, looking solemn.

He hailed a taxi.

'The Buckingham Clinic.'

The clinic was in north London, near the Zoo. A new, white, lavishly glassed building, reflecting autumn's glowing late afternoon. Entering the glittering marbled hall gave him the uneasy feeling of driving past a nasty accident. He was directed to room A16, on the top floor.

A dreadful thing had happened.

The eating, drinking and merrymaking at the Albany skipped along all the livelier from the pursuing shadow with the scythe. The members knew realistically they risked falling any lunchtime into the hands of the medical profession, escape from which might prove difficult. A week before, news spread along the bar of George rushed from home to hospital with a heart attack. It was received with the phlegm of hearing yet another chum isolated with mumps in the sicker of their prepper.

The white-carpet-tiled top corridor was empty. The door of A16 had unlit red and white lights above. Aubrey knocked timorously.

Silence.

Gently he opened the door. He stuck his healthy, ruddy face round the jamb.

He gasped, appalled.

George lay asleep in Marks and Spencer's pyjamas, looking awful.

The patient abruptly opened his eyes.

'Aubrey!'

'George!'

Aubrey came in, all smiles.

'How kind of you to visit me.'

Voice weaker, thought Aubrey. Gosh.

'We were very concerned in the club, old man. It came up at yesterday's committee. Dear old George, languishing in hospital! Somebody must visit him. I got the job.'

'Why?'

'They thought I'd cheer you up.' He started on the task: 'You're looking very well.'

'I've had a severe heart attack,' George told him bleakly.

'I mean . . . you're looking very well for someone who's had a severe heart attack.'

George's arm languishing on the white bed-cover grabbed Aubrey's expensively-tailored sleeve.

'You noticed a change in me, didn't you? Yes, you did! I saw it in your face. Remember Tolstoy's story? *The Death of Ivan Illych*. The sick man's brother-in-law came to stay. His first look – his strangled exclamation – told poor Ivan Illych the worst.'

'Gloomy lot, these Russians,' Aubrey observed.

'If you can't be gloomy about death, you can't be gloomy about anything.'

Feeling it time to change the subject, Aubrey beamed 'From the committee,' and offered from his briefcase a bottle labelled 'Albany Club Brandy'.

George recoiled as from a hissing viper.

'Not a drop!'

Aubrey was shocked. 'What, you?'

'The doctor's forbiddden it.'

'That's a laugh.'

'Laugh?' George was offended.

Aubrey smiled fraternally: 'I mean, I don't think anyone in the club's ever seen you without a glass in your hand.'

'I suppose they're saying drink brought on my present misfortune?'

Aubrey never recalled George so gloomy, even after Vanessa had left him. Though members whose wives walked out generally seemed unusually jolly.

'Oh, I wouldn't go as far as that,' he said awkwardly.

'I bet they are,' George told him firmly from the piled pillows. 'When anyone dies, they always mutter: "Well, he shifted it a bit, didn't he?" They don't really like the idea of other members dying. The bell tolls for all mankind. They prefer to provide people with a decent excuse.'

Aubrey felt it time to suggest: 'Mind if I have a quick one?' He upturned an empty glass on the bedside locker with the telephone and console of switches. 'Anything nasty been in this?'

'Our dear old club!' George gave a long sigh while Aubrey gurgled brandy from the bottle. '"This smelly, tawny, male paradise", as a member once called the better one. With the big clock on top. In Westminster.'

Aubrey raised his glass.

'To our dear old club!'

'I suppose the clubs are London's most comfortable old folks' day centres,' George reflected less miserably.

'To the ignorant public, they're haunts of the privileged rich.'

'But Aubrey, dear boy, you *are* the privileged rich.'

'Sure you wouldn't like a drop?'

'You wish to kill me,' George asserted quietly.

'But you've recovered,' Aubrey encouraged him.

George shook his head. 'You never recover from a heart attack. One day I shall have another. This is the first shovelfuls of my grave.'

'My dear chap!'

Aubrey became impatient. 'You must look on the bright side.'

'What bright side? I don't care for the whole idea.

Oscar Wilde called being dead the most boring thing in life except having lunch with a schoolmaster. I believe he said it posthumously.'

On the table spanning the bed lay a book with a dog-eared jacket proclaiming '*The Fling of Youth*, A Novel By George Gifford'.

'My first,' George informed Aubrey as he picked it up.

'Got the same photo on the jacket as your last,' Aubrey noticed.

'Publishers are very economical about such things.'

'But think! You must have given a lot of pleasure to a lot of people.'

'The same could be said about a lot of ladies in Soho.' George reached for a glass of barley water. 'What a trivial occupation for a man's whole existence! You see the truth when your life's brought sharply into focus. I find it very, very sad.'

George replaced the empty glass and began quietly to cry.

Aubrey felt dreadfully uncomfortable.

'Please don't blub,' he implored. 'It embarrasses me.'

He passed a box of tissues, trying not to look.

'The club sent you to cheer me up.' George wiped his eyes. 'Well, get on with it.'

'I heard a terribly funny story in the bar the other day,' Aubrey continued more hopefully. 'Trouble is, I've forgotten it.'

The door flew open and one of the prettiest girls Aubrey had seen for ages burst in.

2

'Good afternoon, Mr Gifford,' said the nurse chirpily. 'Like to order your supper?'

'I've ordered it.'

'For two days' time, Mr Gifford. The kitchen has to have notice.'

'Two days! I could then be dining on Olympus.'

'Sorry?' she puzzled. She read from a typed list: 'There's prawn cocktail or chilled melon *suprème de volaille* or plaice mornay ice-cream or gâteau.'

'You choose. You know the difference between them.'

'You're very naughty about your diet, Mr Gifford. Now it's time for your obs.'

As deftly as a ballet dancer, she took thermometer from tube on the wall, inserted it under George's tongue, clasped his wrist, and upturned towards her grave eyes the watch on her bosom.

Aubrey appreciatively inspected from his chair her white-stretched rear, his eye reaching down to her black stockings and up to the dark curls under her perched white cap.

'Lovely, Mr Gifford.' She shook and replaced the instrument. 'And the bowels, Mr Gifford?'

'Most definitely.'

'Lovely. Thank you, Mr Gifford.'

She vanished.

'Dreadfully young,' reflected Aubrey.

'You get used here to being treated like a child by children.'

'This place must cost the earth.'

'Oh, yes. Only the Arabs can afford its more expensive operations.'

Aubrey stood to stare through the window.

'Well, you get a splendid view for your money. I do believe I can actually see the club. They'll just be sitting down among the leather and brass fenders for their tea and anchovy toast,' he depicted fondly.

'The judges hot from the Old Bailey,' George said dreamily. 'The MPs rousing for a night's sleepwalking through the lobbies. The journalists sobering up from lunch.'

'I adore anchovy toast,' Aubrey recalled with relish.

'Best thing in the club,' George agreed. 'The rest of the food's as bad as here.'

'I don't know,' Aubrey objected thoughtfully. 'I love the prunes and custard. And the rice pudding. The Irish stew on Mondays is excellent.'

'Schoolboy grub,' George dismissed it.

'We're all schoolboys there, aren't we?' Aubrey said tenderly. 'That's the delight and wonder of the place.'

He sat down again. 'Wish I could remember that funny story. It was about a Frenchman.'

He refreshed his glass and flourished the bottle.

'Come on! Just a little drop. It'll put the smile back on your face.'

'Remember Apthorpe,' George said doomfully.

Aubrey frowned. 'In the club?'

'In Evelyn Waugh. The hero of *Men at Arms* smuggled a bottle of whisky into Apthorpe's bed in a military hospital. It killed him. There was a terrible row. He was expelled from the regiment.'

Aubrey laughed. 'I don't think I'd be expelled from the club.'

George said sharply: 'So if I succumbed to your importunate temptation, *you'd* be all right?'

'You *are* tetchy this afternoon,' Aubrey complained crossly. 'Not your usual self in the bar. Always so full of merry quips.'

George told him softly: 'I've already been dead, of course.'

'What!'

'Oh, yes. In and out of the Pearly Gates.'

Aubrey looked confused. 'I don't follow, old man.'

George grabbed his sleeve again.

'Do you know how it all started? I'd been to the club for lunch. Going home on the bus, I got this terrible pain, here in the breastbone. I thought it was indigestion. It was Thursday, tripe and onions day, to which I'm very partial. In my flat, I'd the terrifying feeling of my chest being crushed by some huge vice. I struggled to the phone, rang my doctor. She instantly called an ambulance, sent me here. The National Health Service is impossible, of course, you read things in the papers, probably have to share a bed. I arrived, flashing blue lights, you know, sirens, whooo-whooo. Then guess what happened?'

Aubrey sat open-mouthed. 'No idea.'

'My heart stopped.'

'No!'

'Like that.' George snapped his fingers. 'I was dead. As a doornail.'

'You poor fellow,' said Aubrey with concern. 'Did it hurt?'

'Luckily, they've wonderful machines. The doctors start your heart with electricity, easy as starting their cars. I came to, with wires and tubes leading from me everywhere. I looked like a sea anemone.'

'Amazing!'

'Happening all over these days,' George told him casually. 'Everybody's Lazarus now.'

Aubrey looked intent. 'Must be very interesting, dying.'

'Nothing to it. I saw a great flashing light, like the sun exploding. Next thing, the nurse was telling me to stop biting her finger.'

'You may have looked upon the face of God,' suggested Aubrey reverently.

'I've a dreadful memory for faces.'

'I always imagined God as a rather crusty but very decent member of the Albany, with a beard.'

'An improvement on him in stained glass.'

'Come to think of it, I've always imagined Heaven as the club bar – serving drinks that made you tiddly but never pissed, free of charge, naturally – with Lord's cricket ground outside staging an eternal Test.'

'I'm thirsty.'

George picked an empty jug from the locker.

'Ring for nurse, there's a good chap, Aubrey. No, no, not that one! It sets off bells, red lights. It's for having another heart attack.'

'I say–!'

Aubrey noticed a small bedside television screen, covered with lively wiggles.

'It's my electrocardiograph.'

'But how fascinating!'

George opened his pyjamas, displaying three leads running from circular pads across his chest. 'I'm wired up, day and night.'

'You mean, all those funny little humps and dumps are your heart working?'

'That's right,' George said proudly. 'They tell me one now goes the wrong way, or something. When I was dead downstairs the line was as flat as a floorboard.'

Aubrey sat on the edge of the bed. 'I could sit watching it for ages. Much more interesting than the telly.'

Nurse swept in.

'Want a bottle, do you, Mr Gifford?'

She thrust at George this famous piece of hospital furniture.

'No, I want some barley water.'

'I'm sure you want a bottle,' she corrected him. 'If you don't use a bottle now, you'll want to use a bottle soon, won't you?'

She inserted it firmly under the bedclothes.

'There you are, Mr Gifford. You'll feel much better if you use a bottle. Will your visitor wait outside, please?'

'Oh, we often pee together,' Aubrey told her.

'Sorry?'

'In the club. Behind Mr Gladstone.'

'Sorry?'

'I can't do anything,' George confessed.

'Do try, Mr Gifford.'

She left.

Hands under bedclothes, George screwed up his face. 'Still can't.'

'Why bother, old man?'

'But I'll so upset the dear girl if I don't.'

George held his breath. 'Help me, dear boy?'

'Me?'

'Whistle.'

'Whistle?'

'Works like a charm with children.'

Aubrey tunelessly whistled the National Anthem.

'Released the flood?' he asked solicitously.

George shook his head.

'Shall I try another tune?'

He rendered *Greensleeves*.

George suggested: 'Knock on something. That's supposed to be equally evocative.'

Aubrey drummed a fruit-knife on the locker, whistling the Marseillaise.

'I know! I'll turn on the tap.'

Aubrey ran the swan-necked tap of the corner washbasin for some time, with an enquiring look. George shook his head. Aubrey sat down again and poured another brandy.

'In the great days of London clubs,' he dissertated, 'in the eighteenth century, when the members did nothing but drink and gamble by candlelight, at White's they had page-boys to duck under the card table with potties, so gentlemen needn't interrupt their game.'

'Most London clubs – like ours – are shams, aren't they?' George continued to look preoccupied. 'Victorian imitations.'

'Like most public schools.'

'But we spend so much of our national life – constitutional, legal, religious, architectural, commercial – enjoying the Victorian reproduction of the mediaeval.'

'Why not? That's our debt to the Victorians. They knew how to make themselves comfortable.'

Aubrey fell silent. How sad, seeking to console stricken George in such glacially uncongenial surroundings! Perhaps the poor man would do better in the club, tucked with a rug into his favourite chair in the morning room, his feet on a gout-stool and Brindles bringing unending pinkers.

'Finished, Mr Gifford?'

The nurse rushed in, lifted the bedclothes and whipped out the bottle, interrupting George's triumphant peeing noise.

3

'The doctor will be here soon, Mr Gifford,' said nurse, leaving with the bottle. 'He's going to tell you when you can go home isn't he? That'll be nice, won't it?'

'They enquire into your domestic circumstances,' said George dourly as the door shut. 'I haven't had any domestic circumstances for years.'

Aubrey stuck out his feet, relaxed with his brandy.

'You know, everyone at the club was very surprised when Vanessa left you.'

'Everyone at the club saw her only safely caged in the ladies' dining room.'

'We all thought you'd done pretty well for yourself, old boy, as a matter of fact. A sexy young wife, at your age.'

'Well, she was blonde,' George conceded. 'It is a widespread mistake to correlate the brilliance of the hair with that of the performance.'

'Do you ever see her?'

'Oh, no. She went off with various people. I suppose she found them more inspiring than me. You see, we *both* made a mistake. She thought a novelist was something romantic. I always remember what Elizabeth Jenkins wrote about Ouida – you know, *Under Two Flags*. "The lives of imaginative writers are the wrong side of the carpet, all blurs and knots with ends of thread hanging out; the true pattern is on the other side, in their work." Who'd like to be in bed with a rolled-up Wilton?'

'She knows you're ill?'

'Yes. I sent her a postcard.'

'Sent one back?'

'No. But I suppose an ex-wife must retain *some* interest in the flesh she was once part of.'

'You've no one else?'

George shook his head. 'You know I live alone.'

He added pathetically: 'That's why I'm so often in the club. Any company's better than my own.'

Aubrey looked concerned. 'When they let you out of this lazar-house, I suppose you can cope?'

'A lady cleans. Food you buy appetizingly packaged for instant enjoyment, like paperbacks.'

'Shouldn't you go and recuperate somewhere? People always do in novels.'

'I once read in a book of the thirties – Connolly, I expect – "the best novels are written in cheap hotel bedrooms in the South of France." Now, of course, you can't even find a cheap sandwich in the South of France. But I managed a winter there, writing that–'

George indicated the book on the bed-table.

'With the Alpes Maritimes looking over my shoulder, I felt a definite literary ambience. If I got on a chair, I could see Somerset Maugham's villa through my window.'

He smiled nostalgically. 'I can still smell the garlic, the fresh croissants, the coffee, the pissoirs. Stinks are much more potent than Noël Coward's cheap music. So I'm going back, soon as the doctor gives me *congé*. To rewrite that novel – as I'd write it today.'

'Seems a good idea,' Aubrey said encouragingly.

'It's a bloody stupid idea.'

'Your public will love it,' he insisted.

'Do you realize that the average author's public is as exclusive as the average chess champion's?'

'But George! You have a great literary reputation.'

'Once, people Dorothy Parker called "the booksie-wooksies" found me a promising young author. Then I became a promising middle-aged author. Now I'm a promising senile author.'

'Senile? You're no older than me.'

'This kicks away a few arches of your lifespan.' George patted his electronically observed chest. 'I shan't – unlike you, dear boy – enjoy the seventh age, stuffed with hearing-aids, pacemakers and other gadgets, like the modern home.'

Aubrey said consolingly: 'I might get a heart attack, too. Does that cheer you up?'

'You might,' George informed him cheerfully. 'I've learned a lot about it. They're common in pink-cheeked, fat, jolly chaps. The doctors call you the pyknic type.'

Aubrey was puzzled. 'Picnic?'

'With a y. Greek. "Forasmuch as all mortal men be subject to many sudden perils, diseases, and sicknesses, and ever uncertain what time they shall depart out of this life; therefore, to the intent they may be always in a readiness to die, whensoever it shall please Almighty God to call them." The Visitation of the Sick. Sound advice.'

'They have a padre here?'

'For all established religions. It's an international clientele. The C of E chap came to see me. Very decent.

Perhaps only because he suspected I'd be shortly talking to them up at Head Office. Cheer me up.'

'That funny story.' Aubrey frowned, trying to remember. 'It's frightfully witty.'

He reached for the brandy bottle.

George stared at the ceiling.

'When I'm dead, the Gallant Winco will put a black-edged sheet on the club noticeboard: "The committee much regrets to announce the death of Mr George Gifford, a member since . . ." God knows when. Our quietus made not with a bare bodkin but a brass thumb-tack.'

'The committee's trying to abolish that rather barbaric custom. In the middle of winter, there's so many names on the board you can hardly read the lunch menu. But a lot of members object.'

'It would never do to spoil their fun.'

George grabbed Aubrey's sleeve, nearly spilling the brandy.

'Do you know why people turn – often first – to the obituaries in the newspapers? Tolstoy again: "The complacent feeling that, 'It is he who is dead and not I' ".'

'George, your uncharacteristic melancholy is becoming boring,' Aubrey told him frankly.

'"In his numerous clubs the politely jocular greetings will be rather more solemn today with his death in mind".'

'What miserable sod wrote that?'

'John Betjeman.'

'He was never a member,' Aubrey said dismissively.

Nurse appeared with a vast, elaborately arranged, carefully wrapped bouquet.

'Somebody's sent you some lovely flowers, Mr Gifford.'

George sat bolt upright from his pillows.

'Me? Sure? Who could possibly send me flowers?'

'Shall I unwrap them for you, Mr Gifford?'

With the practised dexterity which took pulses and temperatures, she began arranging them in the two empty vases.

'Aren't they beautiful, Mr Gifford?'

'They're bloody expensive,' observed Aubrey.

'Vanessa!' George struck fist into palm. 'Why, the old darling. Fancy her, spending good money on a floral display like this.'

'Why, I shall have to fetch another vase, Mr Gifford,' nurse said proudly.

'You see, Aubrey, I was right. A woman never becomes insensitive to any body with which she has enjoyed intimate contact, however brief. Vanessa was a very sympathetic sort, you know. Quite sloppy, in fact. Wept in bed. A woman will seize any irreproachable excuse – like this – to express feelings which she still cherishes towards a man, feelings that have been suppressed by. . . . What? The memories of a row. Bitterness. Or simply the passage of time. Isn't there a card?'

'There you are, Mr Gifford.'

Nurse left.

George squinted at arm's length.

'Where are my glasses? You read it, Aubrey.'

'It says, "Get well soon, with lots of love from . . . Gloria!"'

'Gloria?'

'What's my wife doing, sending you flowers?' Aubrey asked warmly.

'I've no idea,' George told him blankly.

'But she didn't even know you were ill.' He was mystified. 'I just happened to mention this morning that I was coming here to see you.'

'Do thank her for me, won't you?' George invited politely.

'*I* have to pay for them,' Aubrey pointed out.

'Well, it's terribly decent of you.'

Aubrey looked disgusted. 'I was thinking of bringing you some fruit, too. Thank goodness I didn't.'

Nurse reappeared with a cut-glass vase.

'Someone must think a lot of you, Mr Gifford,' she said cosily.

'It *was* a nice gesture of Gloria's.' George contentedly surveyed the crop.

Aubrey said sourly: 'She may send them to *all* members of the Albany in hospital, for what I know.'

'Why not? We're a band of brothers.' It occurred to George: 'When the occasion arises, do you suppose I should entertain the club to a memorial service?'

'Well, you're in the memorial service class.'

George reflected: 'The same chaps seem to attend all of them, irrespective of corpse. They get pissed in the bar at lunchtime as usual, but wearing black ties.'

Aubrey made the practical suggestion: 'You might imitate more generous members, who leave a bequest for a party after their funeral.'

'Melancholy occasions! Even our notorious cadgers of drinks from the living shiver at plucking nosegays from wreaths.'

'There, Mr Gifford.'

The nurse set one vase on the windowsill behind George's head, the others at each end of the table spanning his middle.

'They do brighten the place up, don't they, Mr Gifford? Make you look much more cheerful.'

'They make me look as if I'm lying in state already.'

'Sorry?'

'Frightful bore, visiting the sick, isn't it?' George mentioned as she left. 'Don't let me keep you.'

'I was only going to the club,' Aubrey said vaguely.

He picked up the novel again.

'Did you know, before I went into the City I wrote a little book? Poetry. No one published it, of course. I hadn't the confidence – the cheek – to try. I've still got it at home. Would you like to see it?'

'Not really.'

Aubrey replaced it with a shrug.

'Why fart about with verse, when you can be a successful stockbroker? Aubrey–'

George paused, so long that Aubrey's eyes strayed towards the twitching line on the television screen.

'Do you remember when you dashed to New York, to merge your firm with one of the most thrustful, sharpest, richest stockbrokers on Wall Street?'

'Very well! It was the best deal of my life.'

George raised himself on an elbow.

'Good. Now. Listen–'

The door sprung open. Nurse heralded: 'The doctor.'

4

The doctor was very 'Harley Street'. Tall, tanned, hawk-nosed, lean, closely tailored, he most inconsiderately exuded aggressive health.

'How are you? You look splendid.'

This advertised at once his 'bedside manner'.

'He's getting more cheerful, doctor,' nurse contributed brightly.

'Good!'

The doctor was staring at Aubrey, as if discovering in him some fascinating and serious disease.

'I say! Isn't that an Albany Club tie?'

Aubrey looked down at the purple, magenta and gold stripes.

'Unfortunately, yes.'

'He's on the committee,' George extolled his friend. 'My own five years sitting on it are just up. Remarkable what one heard about one's fellow members.'

The doctor ignored his patient – quite 'unprofessional conduct'.

'*Are* you? On the committee? What an extraordinary coincidence. I'm up for membership. Soon, I believe. Quite imminent. I hope you won't blackball me!'

He laughed, nervously.

'We don't blackball many candidates.' Aubrey was gently elbowing the brandy bottle behind the windowsill flowers. 'You see, we need their money.'

'To be blackballed by a gentlemen's club!'

The doctor looked grave, as if announcing some fatal condition.

'The only humiliation and disgrace left in our modern life to afflict any respectable, successful man. But I suppose once you're in, it's a good way of getting your own back on people you dislike.'

Aubrey said generously: 'Your patient is a pillar of the Albany Club.'

'The Albany Club has more pillars than the Parthenon,' George declared modestly. 'If not so perpendicular.'

'Lindisfarne-Jones is the name, when it comes up,' emphasized the doctor, nurse opening the door to eject Aubrey.

The doctor switched attention to the television screen, pressing switches to 'freeze' the wiggles and do other interesting things.

'A splendid club, the Albany,' he complimented George meanwhile, over his shoulder. 'Many of my private patients say so. Your grouse in season is the best in London, I believe. And the wines! Superb choice, I gather. I do hope no tragedy will prevent our meeting there one day.'

George said gloomily: 'You mean, my dropping dead from another heart attack?'

'Oh, no,' the doctor assured him, intent on the screen. 'If I got blackballed. That T-wave is looking much better today,' he pointed out to nurse.

He pressed a button and gathered a strip like a big supermarket bill.

'You'll never have another heart attack,' he assured George robustly. 'Well, that's the way to look at it, anyway. I want you to put this myocardial infarct right out of your mind.'

He festooned the flower-bedecked bed-table with his streamer.

'See for yourself, how it's healing already. The bit that went up is coming down. I'm extremely satisfied with your trace. Lead a normal life. Just be sensible – no squash tomorrow morning, eh, ha ha! Gentle, progressive exercise is the ticket. Do you walk much?'

'Never, if I can help it.'

'We'll have to change all that, won't we? Buy a stout pair of shoes. There's plenty of interesting walks, right here in London. I expect you've got books about them. When shall we send you home? Tomorrow?'

George looked delighted.

'Oh, we don't keep people in hospital these days. Dreadfully uneconomical. I want your blood. Nurse, a 10 ml syringe, please.'

Aubrey was sitting on a white plastic chair in the corridor when the door opened.

'The doctor's finished,' nurse condescended.

'I hope we three will meet again in more convivial surroundings,' the doctor told Aubrey, squirting George's blood into a bottle.

'I say!' He handed nurse the blood. 'Is that one of your books?'

'Would you like it?' George offered generously.

'But how very kind.'

The doctor picked the novel delicately from the bed-table, as though handling some infected organ.

'I'll sign it for you.'

'Would you? That would be delightful.'

George fumbled for a ballpoint on the locker.

'Er – will you put, "To Penelope"?'

'Penelope?'

'That's my teenage daughter. I'm not a great bookman myself, but I know she'd love to have it on her shelf. Thank you. What splendid flowers! I'm sure you won't mind if I take a buttonhole? Nurse – scissors.'

He snipped.

'See me in Harley Street,' he directed, leaving. 'Three weeks. Meanwhile, keep cheerful.'

He turned at the door to Aubrey.

'Lindisfarne-Jones. Don't forget.'

'It's always for their daughter,' George complained despondently, once the clubmen were alone. 'A literary work autographed by its creator they regard as a Mickey Mouse doll from Disneyland.'

'She will cherish it for life,' Aubrey consoled him. 'You write for posterity.'

'Posterity could begin tomorrow afternoon.'

Aubrey ignored this. 'Did the doctor spot the brandy?'

'I don't think so. He was too busy showing off. I'm going home tomorrow.'

'Splendid, old man! I'll tell them at the club.'

Aubrey picked up his briefcase, inserting the brandy bottle.

'Well. Must be getting along.'

George asked: 'Aubrey, when you were doing that lucrative deal in New York, where was Gloria?'

'In Cannes.'

'With me.'

'What!'

Aubrey glared.

'At that smallish hotel on the Croisette,' George elaborated. 'It was perfectly comfortable.'

Aubrey asked irately: 'What did you do that for?'

'Well. You know.'

'But you only met her in the ladies' dining room,' he objected.

'No. We met once in Harrods. In the food halls.'

Aubrey looked shocked. 'And that decided her to spend a fortnight with you in the South of France?'

'She thought I was romantic. It's a widespread illusion.'

Aubrey gave a deep sigh. He dropped his briefcase on the bed. 'Is this still going on?'

'Oh, no. Not for ages. She came to my flat a few afternoons. Then she went off me. Like Vanessa.'

'What are you telling me this for now?'

'Isn't it traditional to confess our sins in the proximity of death? It provides a cast-iron excuse for delightful irresponsibility.'

George smiled, nestling into the bedclothes.

'I've a wonderful feeling of relief. Better, of smugness. Are you really angry?'

Aubrey paused. He said resignedly: 'How can you be angry with a man who's been dead?'

He opened the briefcase and poured himself another brandy.

'And after all, George, we're members of the same club.'

George unexpectedly laughed. 'Like the old club story? Member phones porter, "Can I share a club bedroom with a lady not my wife? So long as she's the wife of another member, sir".'

'Believe me, at the time I might have been . . . very upset.'

Aubrey gulped brandy.

'But my circumstances, like yours, have changed.'

George looked interested.

'To be frank, I don't give a monkey's about Gloria,' Aubrey continued awkwardly. 'There's been nothing . . . sexual between us for months.'

'You surprise me,' George said drily.

Aubrey shrugged. 'It's not the sort of thing one mentions in the club. And I'm not a plaster saint, you know.'

'Indeed?'

'I met a lady,' he confessed.

'Pretty?'

'Beautiful.'

'Young?'

'Half my age.'

'Congratulations.'

'She works in the City.'

'Sexy?'

'Unbelievable.'

'How delightful.'

'My firm has a flat.'

Aubrey sat down with his glass, relaxed again.

'A flat convenient for the office. For entertaining distinguished visitors. Though not many distinguished visitors see the inside of it. The tax people don't know that.'

'And what does Gloria know?'

'Nothing.'

'It would hurt her,' George said thoughtfully. 'Women particularly dislike a practical demonstration of losing sexual attraction.'

Aubrey said recklessly: 'I don't care.'

'You amaze me.'

'Do I? Why?'

'Because you're terrified of doing anything that might slightly tarnish your ridiculous self-image of a frightfully decent chap.'

Aubrey asked indignantly: 'What gave you that idea?'

'It's been round the club for years,' George told him casually.

Aubrey protested: 'It's certainly news to me.'

'Oh, nobody at the Albany gets the slightest inkling of all the spiteful things said behind their backs. The members are far too tender-hearted towards each other.'

'I wish I hadn't told you now. I don't know why I did. To cheer you up, I suppose.'

'It won't go any further,' George assured him.

'It will! You're the biggest gossip in the club.'

'I'm not!' George disagreed stoutly.

'Of course you are. Absolutely everybody says so. Why do you suppose you find yourself drinking alone in the club bar?'

George suggested vaguely: 'I get there rather early, I suppose.'

'Not a bit! Members spot you through the door, and go and order their drinks from Brindles in the morning room.' Aubrey added brutally: 'You're one of the club bores.'

George was horrified. 'Me? But everyone roars their heads off at my stories.'

'They used to, they used to. In a club, all men become caricatures of themselves. Happens outside, I suppose, but there you can always escape. The talkative become garrulous, the amusing become facetious, the convivial become plain drunks. You're a club bore, George,' he repeated forcefully. 'And it was about time someone had the courage to tell you.'

'But how appalling!'

George stared between the flowers on his bed-table.

'My standing in the club is the only thing that really matters to me,' he said pitifully. 'A novelist, a husband, a lover – adventures in disappointment. The club is the prop of my life. The club is my soul. Though, come to think of it, I despise most of the members. I'm going to cry again.'

Aubrey continued earnestly: 'If that gossip got round London, it could be the death of me. She's got a husband. Har–!'

He broke off. He grinned.

'I remember it! That funny story. Outside a tall apartment block . . . in Paris . . . taxi draws up . . . big, handsome man gets out . . . huge moustache . . . carrying a sword, a scimitar . . . dashes inside . . . runs upstairs . . . bursts open a door . . . young couple on the bed, *in flagrante delicto* . . . plunges sword through both

. . . turns them over . . . and exclaims: "*Mon Dieu! Je me suis trompé l'étage!*"'

Aubrey laughed loudly, slapping his thigh.

'"*Je me suis trompé l'étage!*"' he repeated delightedly. '"I've mistaken the floor!" Mistaken the floor! Don't you think that's terribly funny, George? Don't you, George? George! George!'

But the gentleman was apparently dead.

SEVEN

1

'Very sad, sir,' said Hawkins.

'Very sad, Hawkins,' Aubrey agreed gloomily.

Brindles stood alone in the morning room, presenting a large silver tray covered with glasses of champagne.

From the hall appeared Aubrey, wearing a black tie. Then Gloria in black, elegant as one of Sargent's ladies (as he managed to be both an artist and a gentleman he was a member in the 1900s, his pencil portrait fills the niche outside the card room).

Next the Gallant Winco, already in winter uniform of plain blue suit and RAF tie. And gentlemen with their ladies, all looking politely miserable.

'I could do with a drink.' Aubrey strode purposefully towards Brindles. 'Memorial services aren't the most cheerful way of spending a morning.'

'You had several before we left home,' Gloria told him crisply.

Aubrey was hurt. 'Well, I needed something before delivering a eulogy on the poor chap. I've never been in a pulpit before.'

'And it was a super eulogy, Aubrey,' Rollo complimented him warmly. 'You made him so alive.'

'Thank you,' Aubrey responded solemnly. 'He was a great human. A great friend. A great clubman.'

'So you just said, dear,' remarked Gloria, more sharply. 'It's terribly depressing, having to wait till you're dead to know how nicely people think of you.'

'I put it in your usual tankard, sir.'

'Thank you, Brindles.'

All reached for the tray. More members drifted in,

wearing their black ties and expressions of fitting piety, and reverently helped themselves.

'Rotten day for it,' observed the Gallant Winco.

Gloria shivered. 'Honestly, in church I couldn't help praying for my thermal underwear.'

'Gets damn cold, that place. These affairs come mostly in winter, of course.'

'You're a regular mourner?' Gloria enquired.

'Never miss one,' the Gallant Winco asured her heartily. 'Though they're all the same. Often forget who's dead. All I know, some of 'em die owing club bills going back to half-crowns and ten-bob notes.'

The Gallant Winco reached again for Brindles' bestowal, as Gloria appraised our beloved morning room.

'What an enormous privilege, escaping from the ladies' bit of the club. I quite feel I've intruded among the beer and sweaty jockstraps of some footy changing room,' she expressed her gratitude.

The Gallant Winco wagged his head fondly. 'Number of times he came to me and said, "Winco, when I go, I want a few friends and their ladies in the dear old club, to stand them a final drink." Typical of the feller.'

Bertie speculated: 'What happens to the ashes?'

Aubrey shrugged. 'End up with the widow, I suppose.'

'They come in a plastic thing like a supermarket milk bottle,' Gloria enlightened them.

'He once said he wanted them scattered down the front steps of the club,' Aubrey recalled. 'Do you suppose he was serious?'

Rollo nodded. 'Could be useful. Those steps get damn slippery in icy weather.'

Aubrey became aware of an ungentlemanly commotion at the front door.

'Madam! Can I help you?' Hawkins was demanding bleakly of a small blonde pink lady with big blue eyes, as ageless as a doll, in a pretty flowered dress.

'Oh, God!' She clasped her hands to her face in shame. 'I should have used the ladies' entrance.'

Hawkins softened. 'It's quite in order this morning, madam. Ladies are permitted through the gentlemen's entrance after memorial services.'

'Memorial services!' She stood horrorstruck upon the chessboard flooring. 'I think I'm the widow!' she cried, rushing into the morning room, throwing herself into Aubrey's arms and bursting into tears.

'Vanessa!' exclaimed Aubrey.

'Aubrey!' exclaimed Vanessa. 'My George! He's dead!'

'But Vanessa–'

'I was in Spain,' she poured out. 'When I got home I found this postcard. Saying he'd this terrible heart attack. I rushed to his flat. All locked up. I rushed to his club. Now it's his memorial service. Poor, poor, darling George! I should never have left him. I'm utterly wretched.'

She sobbed piercingly.

'Vanessa,' Aubrey put her right. 'You've got the wrong party. It's Cuthbert who's dead.'

Her big blue eyes stared from his embrace. 'Who?'

'Cuthbert Cramphorn,' Aubrey explained. 'He was senior partner of my stockbroking firm in the City. That's the widow over there, drinking champagne under Lord Curzon. Great old boy, actually put me up for the club,' he reflected affectionately. 'He was pushing eighty-five when his sight failed. Dreadfully tragic. Tripped over his guide dog and broke his neck.'

'Oh,' said Vanessa. She arranged her tangled thoughts and smoothed her ruffled emotions. 'Then where's George?'

'Convalescing in Sussex on a health farm.'

'Oh,' said Vanessa.

'Have a glass of champagne,' Aubrey invited.

'Sorry you were so upset, Vanessa,' Gloria said gently.

'It doesn't matter,' she reassured them both. 'Now I

know he's not dead, I'm not sure I like him so much.'

'If he had died, we should of course have given a party for *him* in the club,' Aubrey assured her warmly. 'Even if I had to foot the bill.'

'Well, perhaps dear George *should* have died,' Vanessa suggested wistfully sipping champers. 'All the critics seem keen on it. He's the oldest promising novelist in the business. When he was thirty, some beastly reviewer said what a pity he hadn't died at twenty. I expect when he was forty, they said he should have snuffed it at thirty. If he was dead, he might even make some money.'

'George always complains that being a novelist is like Oscar Wilde said about landowning – it gives one position, and prevents one from keeping it up,' Aubrey consoled her. 'Though he always very decently donates signed copies of his works to the club library. Unfortunately, they're always pinched.'

Gloria remarked briskly: 'Surely everybody regards books as things which you beg, borrow or steal, and only buy to give as Christmas presents?'

'I bought George's latest one,' Vanessa said nostalgically. 'It had that lovely photograph of him on the jacket. It must have been taken years ago. Before I left him. Before I met him, I think. All that time we lived together, I'm sure the club gave George more pleasure than I did,' she confessed generously, looking round.

Aubrey raised his silver tankard towards the corner. 'That was George's favourite chair. I see him sitting in it still.'

'Aubrey!' Gloria checked him sharply. 'George is *not* dead. On the contrary, he's on a *health* farm. You usually don't get so maudlin so early in the party.'

Brindles intruded welcomely with the champagne bottle.

Aubrey shortly found himself wedged with Vanessa between Lord Curzon and the bum-warmer.

'But what actually happened to George's poor heart?' she enquired, big blue eyes fixing him over her 'bubbly'.

'Poor chap had a second attack. In hospital. Almost finished him off.'

'How awful!'

'The doctor had just left, but rushed back when the heart-attack alarm went off. Saved him in the nick of time. Good job,' Aubrey reflected thoughtfully. 'The doctor's up for the club, and would certainly be black-balled if George had died.'

'How terrifying!'

'Do you know, I was actually talking to George when it struck him?'

'What about?' she invited.

'I was cheering him up with a joke I'd heard in the club.'

'Share it with me,' she enticed.

'Well, there was this Frenchman, who gets from a taxi outside a big block of flats – in Paris, of course – carrying a huge, naked sword –'

'But you could never go about Paris with a sword. You know how jumpy the police are. George always expected them to start shooting everyone in sight. He said it was like Sydney Smith always expecting dogs to go mad.'

Aubrey persisted: 'Well, this chap did. He was a very big, handsome Frenchman. With a huge moustache.'

'Oooo!' said Vanessa.

'He ran upstairs, kicked open a flat door, found a young couple on the bed – you know – and plunged his sword right through them. Both of them. Like that.'

Vanessa squeezed tight her big blue eyes.

'Then he turned them over and exclaimed: "*Mon Dieu! Je me suis trompé l'étage.*" Which means: "I have mistaken the floor".'

Silence.

'That's all?'

'Yes.'

'That isn't very funny.'

Aubrey looked his most miserable of the morning.

'Don't you think so?'

'I can't see it mattered which floor they were on.'

Aubrey agreed sadly: 'Perhaps George didn't think it funny, either. Though I expect in the fuss he forgot it.'

Brindles asked: 'More champagne, sir? And I was really sorry about poor Sir Cuthbert, sir.'

He upended napkin-shrouded bottle into Aubrey's tankard.

'I'm sure he'll be happy in heaven, sir,' Brindles reassured Aubrey kindly. 'He was the sort of gentleman who'd be happy anywhere.'

'Thank you, Brindles. At least, he'll be among plenty of friends.'

'Indeed, this is a well-upholstered departure lounge from life,' Gloria murmured, returning from inspecting Mr Kipling and Turner's whisky advertisement.

'I always say, madam, when a member dies, he'll make some gentleman – or perhaps some lady, madam – very happy in heaven tonight,' Brindles cheered her.

'You're always so good for George.' Vanessa fixed Gloria with the big blue eyes. 'In his terrible attacks of black gloom. When we still shared the same duvet, just talking about you seemed to cheer him up.'

Gloria was ostentatiously puzzled. 'But I hardly know your husband, Vanessa. Aubrey's his drinking companion in this place. I only meet him in the ladies' dining room.'

'Vanessa!'exclaimed Rollo.

'Rollo!' exclaimed Vanessa. 'And Bertie! How lovely to see you again! How wonderful about George! Not dead in the slightest. Though I don't expect he's much enjoying living on grated carrot and lemon juice, or whatever they give you on these masochistic health farms.'

Aubrey and Gloria were alone under Lord Curzon's nose.

Aubrey silently blew out his cheeks. Gloria perceived that he had something on his mind. This always depressed her.

'You sent an enormously elaborate bunch of flowers to George in hospital,' said Aubrey resolutely. 'It was lucky he survived that second heart attack. Frightful waste of money otherwise.'

He stuck out his tankard to Brindles for more champagne.

2

'And you didn't know George well?' Aubrey reminded her, helping himself to the *canapés*.

'Doesn't everybody send people flowers when they're ill?' Gloria suggested reasonably. 'It's a politeness. Like praying for them.'

Aubrey asked: 'What about Harrods food halls?'

She was perplexed. 'I only go there because of your addiction to Gentleman's Relish.'

'You met George in Harrods food halls once, didn't you?'

'Did I?'

'George told me. When I visited him in that horrible hospital. Surrounded by your flowers.'

Gloria asked peevishly: 'Well, what of it? People shop in Harrods because it's a club for the well-off, like this.'

Aubrey gulped his champagne.

'In Harrods food halls, my dear, you and George arranged to spend a week in Cannes together when I was on business in New York.'

Gloria was outraged.

'What utter nonsense!'

Aubrey transfixed her with a glance like a cocktail stick through a sausage.

'He was in between heart attacks. George had actually died, you know. His heart had stopped. The doctors started it again. They've wonderful machines. Human jump-leads. If you can't believe a man in such circumstances, you can't believe him about anything all his life.'

Gloria gave in. 'Well, all right. Yes. I did.' She clutched the hand holding the tankard. 'Oh, I'm sorry, darling. Are you very, very hurt?'

'It's only our being members of the same club which hurts,' Aubrey told her stiffly.

'I expect it's always happening,' she suggested cordially. 'Women are so segregated from the members here, as though you don't trust yourselves against committing rape.'

He enquired tetchily: 'But how could you enjoy it with *George*? He told me that Vanessa left him because he was on and off like a sparrow on a bird bath.'

'It was a lapse. An adventure. It meant nothing, nothing, emotionally. And I was dreadfully remorseful afterwards. Honestly, darling. If the poor man *had* died, it would hardly seem to matter now, would it?'

'Death may conveniently cancel our tiresome engagements, but not our irritating behaviour.'

'How could anyone be jealous of a corpse?' she objected impatiently. 'It's abnormal. Perfectly Dracula.'

'I remember how George used to quote Balzac: "When a woman comes to repent of a weakness she passes a sponge as it were over her life in order to wipe everything out".'

'I deserve everything except pomposity,' she told him shortly. 'Being found out is shame-making enough. You needn't rub it in.'

'Champagne, sir?'

'Better get another dozen bottles up, Brindles. Si

Cuthbert would be dreadfully annoyed if we didn't do it properly.'

'Very good, sir.'

Aubrey reflected: 'Pity George missing all this fun and vintage champers. Old Cuthbert so disliked the club economy champagne, he wouldn't even order it in his grave.'

He waved his tankard towards George's favourite chair.

'How could you do a sneaky thing like that on me, George?' he demanded. 'Rotter.'

'Darling, why in this alcoholic monastery must you revert to playing schoolboys?'

'That's how a bunch of men always get on together. Whoever heard of a bunch of women happily being schoolgirls?'

'Women are more emotionally mature. We have to give birth.'

'You don't understand. We all share the same pair of hairbrushes, you know, in the loo.'

'Are you comparing me to a hairbrush?'

'That was unnecessary,' he told her sternly. 'We miss each other terribly when we die. I was sure in that awful hospital George was a goner. I felt dreadfully guilty for exciting him with that funny story about the Frenchman.'

'But you're always telling me how somebody or other in the club has behaved abominably. That poor man Willi. I'm sure he's perfectly inoffensive at home.'

'Oh, we may sometimes be a bit prickly. But a hedgehogs' nest is the cosiest place on earth to other hedgehogs.'

'I suppose you've come to know each other's fleas,' she conceded.

As the party gained momentum, there seemed no reason why it should be stopped. Other members passed through the morning room into lunch, the presence of ladies outragedly raising an eyebrow, the explanation sorrowfully shaking a head.

By mid-afternoon, everyone was drunk.

'Brindles, better bring up another dozen champers,' Aubrey ordered vaguely.

'Very good, sir. Sir Cuthbert always did enjoy a good party, didn't he, sir?'

'I must go to the ladies' ladies,' Gloria announced.

'Just past Mr Disraeli, madam.'

Vanessa came close to Aubrey, against Lord Curzon.

'Vanessa–'

She raised her big blue eyes.

'I've something terrible to tell you.'

'Really?' she asked excitedly.

'Your husband seduced my wife Gloria in Cannes.'

Vanessa laughed heartily.

'I mean, it's terrible for me. We're members of the same club.'

'The Gloria Club.'

'Please!

He paused.

'Vanessa–'

She paused.

'Yes?'

'I always enjoyed meeting you terribly, you know. When George brought you to dinner.'

She looked astonished.

'*Did* you?'

'I envy George. Not his intellect, his culture, his fame as a novelist. But for once possessing you.'

'Flatterer.'

'I'm deadly serious,' he corrected her. 'To me, you're the most desirable woman who ever crossed the threshold of the ladies' dining room.'

He wedged her closer against Lord Curzon. 'Are you going back to George? When he's home from Sussex at the end of the month?'

'No,' she decided. 'I think he'd be much better off with the district nurse.'

Aubrey hesitated. 'Does he give you any money?'

'Not a bean.'

'What do you live on, then?'

'Helping out in an antique boutique in Fulham.'

Aubrey said defensively: 'We're not a lot of insensitive old buffers here, you know. We often have a whip-round for impoverished widows.'

'How sweet.'

He assured her warmly: 'Luckily, George is alive and well and performing all those exercises girls do on TV. Enjoying weightlifting, too, for all I know.'

'I'm sure his heart attack's done him a lot of good.'

Aubrey continued with off-hand modesty: 'I suppose I'm pretty well off. Much better off, if it weren't for Gloria's tastes,' he added unsportingly. 'If I could be of any help to you with . . . say . . . well . . . a thousand?'

She smiled and stroked his cheek. Her big blue eyes suggested that she knew the gentlemanly game.

The Gallant Winco lurched between them.

'Long past lunchtime. Getting the chef to send up some cold grouse.'

Aubrey said enthusiastically: 'Good idea! Cuthbert loved grouse. So does George, of course,' he added to Vanessa.

'And a Stilton. Barrel of Bath Olivers. Some port.'

'The Warre's '63,' Aubrey reminded him. 'Memorial services count as birthdays.'

The Gallant Winco lurched away again.

'Why don't the two of us have dinner in the ladies' dining room, very soon, to discuss it?'

Vanessa smiled wider and stroked his cheek.

She said softly: 'That would be very nice.'

Gloria returned from Mr Disraeli and they started talking about the rugger at Twickers.

3

With their customary admirable and charming gallantry, when the members of the Albany Club decided to open a ladies' dining room they created it wholeheartedly feminine.

The wallpaper had huge roses, the windows had chintz curtains and the chairs chintz seats, the little round tables had pink frilly cloths and vases filled with pretty flowers.

Vanessa sat down with Aubrey.

'How lovely! Back in this delicious hyped-up tearoom.'

'I'm so glad you were free for dinner tonight.'

He guardedly inspected the other members and their ladies.

'Do you know, Aubrey, when I walked out on George, the first thing I thought as the front door slammed behind me?'

'Now I don't need to read any more of his novels?'

'No. Now I've resigned from the Albany Club. It was a distinct disadvantage.'

Aubrey leant across the pink candle flickering in a glass funnel.

'I told Gloria I was dining at my club. She assumes I'm having a jolly time with the boys.'

'How deceitful of you.'

'After all, I hadn't a hint what she was up to in Cannes with George.'

'But my dear, isn't it a shade risky?'

Vanessa's eyes followed his sweeping the room.

'You could easily have taken me to some fashionable restaurant.'

'In a fashionable restaurant I could meet any of Gloria's friends. She'd know about it before we got to the *soufflé*. Here I meet only my own.'

'But they all know who I am. And you said they gossip like a typing pool.'

He reassured her: 'There's nothing in the slightest improper about my comforting the lady of a sick member. And of course the staff are terribly, terribly discreet,' he added, as Brindles approached with the leatherbound wine list.

'Good evening, sir.'

'Good evening, Brindles. We'll start with a bottle of champagne.'

Brindles was astounded.

'But you never have champagne at dinner with madam, sir.'

'Bollinger,' Aubrey said firmly.

'Very good, sir.'

Brindles was replaced by Rosie, our 'nippy'.

Aubrey picked up the typed menu card in its silver clip.

'Let us roister with the oyster, in the shorter days and moister,' he suggested to Vanessa waggishly.

'Mmmmmm!' she agreed.

'George quotes that every time he eats them. I think we're all getting a teeny bit bored with it. Two dozen Whitstables, Rosie.'

She looked from her pad, amazed.

'*Two* dozen, Mr Whitaker? Oh, yes, sir,' she corrected herself. 'It's madam who can't eat oysters.'

'This madam does,' Aubrey told her shortly.

He apologized as Rosie left: 'The staff become rather preoccupied with the members' habits. A good fault, I suppose.'

Vanessa lowered her voice. 'The whole room is looking at me out of the corner of its eye.'

'I said not to worry. You're the lady of a member.'

'Tell me, darling, in the rules is wife-swapping permitted or obligatory?'

'The members will perfectly well understand my dining you, while George is a stricken man.'

'You're always talking about George,' she complained, pouting. 'He means much more to you than he does to me.'

'It's just that George is part of the club, whether he's here or doing push-ups in Sussex.'

They paused for Brindles to pop the cork and pour.

She observed: 'George seems to be buying me a hell of a lot of surrogate champagne.'

Aubrey raised a sparkling glass.

'To you. To us.'

She enquired: 'Why are you so *avid* to sleep with me?'

He considered. 'I always admired you so enormously, Vanessa. Then you came back to enlighten my life through George's unfortunate brush with death.'

'Well, darling, I had the weeniest suspicion you were treating me as your last chance saloon.'

'I don't follow?'

She sipped champagne, elbows on table, glass between hands.

'There's a well-known masculine condition. Terror at the shutting of life's doors. The Germans have a word for it. *Torschlusspanik*.'

Aubrey looked mystified. 'Doubtless.'

'So . . . there's a tendency among men for final fun before the clang resounds in the ears.'

Aubrey now looked uncomfortable. 'You mean, I might drop dead any minute, like George nearly did?'

'Oh, no, darling, but . . well, we don't die all of a piece, do we? Bits wear out first.'

'Oh! I see.' Aubrey blew out his cheeks. He complained morosely: 'How can you suggest something like that? I'm sure George would be terribly upset, if he got to hear.'

Vanessa put down her champagne.

'Well, let's put it to the practical test, then, shall we?'

It took some seconds to sink in.

Aubrey exclaimed: 'Vanessa! Darling! Wonderful! How wonderful!'

He reached to clutch her across the table, but remembering where he was sat on his hands instead.

He imparted fervently: 'I wish I could take you to Cannes. Which would jolly well serve Gloria right.'

'Haven't you a room for this sort of thing in the club?'

'Where do you live?' he asked eagerly.

'To save money, with my sister and her husband in Ladbroke Grove.'

'I'm sure her husband would be accommodating?'

'Her husband is the Vicar of Ladbroke Grove.'

'Oh. Let's think. My stockbroking firm has a flat near the City. For important overseas visitors. Though it's mostly used by the partners after banquets and . . . well.'

She said obligingly: 'Thursday afternoon. It's my antique shop's early closing.'

'This Thursday afternoon?'

'If you like.'

Aubrey confided earnestly: 'You've made me the happiest man in the club.'

'I'm glad. Here's the oysters.'

'You did get my cheque at your shop, didn't you?'

'Oh, yes. Thanks.'

4

'You're late, dear.'

Aubrey yawned deeply.

'Met some fellows in the club. Interesting, actually. One was a judge. Another a bishop. Another a headmaster.'

The Whitakers had a flat north of the Park.

Gloria lay in a filmy 'nightie' against the pillows watching the late-night 'movie'.

She smiled admiringly.

'Keeping respectable company.'

'The club, you know,' Aubrey said vaguely.

He shed his jacket and wandered absently round their stylish bedroom, with Brussels blinds.

'Which bishop was it? You once introduced me to a bishop in the ladies' dining room. I was frightfully impressed. It was like meeting God himself.'

'Cirencester. The big, fat one, who's hot on the virgin birth.'

Aubrey sat on a brocade chair and loosened his shoes.

'What did you have for dinner, dear?'

'The usual leg of pork. Decanter of dreadful club claret. Inevitable scotch woodcock. They really should provide something better, or at least different. But I suppose we dine there to stimulate the brain, not the appetite.'

'What about the bores?'

'Oh, they were at the end of the table tonight, boring each other.'

'So you enjoyed yourself?'

'But you know I always enjoy myself at the club.'

Gloria said casually: 'I often wonder, darling, when you say you're at the club whether you're out with another woman.'

Aubrey was appalled.

'What! Me? Oh, no. Perish the thought.'

'Indeed, I often wonder if the popularity of gentlemen's clubs is giving the gentlemen the excuse for doing exactly that.'

'Oh, come. Come, come!'

He removed his Hawes & Curtis shirt. He looked pained.

'Why should you suddenly think that of me?'

Her eyes were still on the television.

'Two reasons. Both very human. Getting your own back, now you know about me and George in Cannes–'

'Oh, come, come, come!'

'Secondly, you're getting on a bit, darling, aren't you? Life's doors are starting to shut. That's just when a lot of men panic, and make fools of themselves.'

Aubrey's mouth opened.

'Where did you hear all that rubbish?'

'Oh, some friend's psychiatrist.'

'Did you know, there's a special German word for it? *Torschlusspanik*,' he told her off-handedly.

'Really? Where did you hear *that*?'

'Oh, tonight. At the club. The bishop. He was rabbiting on about it.'

'So if you want to chance your arm with some little floozie before it's too late, darling, I'm hardly in a position to object, am I?'

Aubrey enquired innocently: 'Floozie?'

Gloria was more interested in herself than her rivals.

'Strange how George exposed my murky past. You know, I really wouldn't have thought it of him. After all, I got to know him pretty well at Cannes. I sent him those lovely flowers, too.'

Aubrey said pointedly: 'Poor George was a very good friend of mine at the club.'

'If I had to choose between betraying my club and betraying my friend's wife, I hope I should have the guts to betray my friend's wife,' she wittily misquoted D. M. Forster (never a member, for obvious reasons).

Aubrey countered: 'I always thought the original was a bloody stupid remark.'

Gloria mentioned: 'How's Vanessa coping?'

'Vanessa? Wouldn't know. Not the slightest idea. Why do you ask?'

'Well, dear, we all know that George as an author is intellectual rather than profitable. I doubt if he gives her a penny. I rather suspected the other day she might be exploiting George's friendship to get her hands on some of yours.'

Aubrey dismissed this cheerfully. 'Well, I've never seen anyone so enjoy a memorial service.'

'Oh, she's a dreadfully vulgar woman. God knows why George married her.'

Gloria flicked off the film and snuggled into bed.

She observed sleepily: 'I always felt that any man who had sex with Vanessa was capable of chucking a brick through a Picasso. Have you put the cat out?'

5

Aubrey bounded up the club steps.

'Good morning, Hawkins!'

'Good morning, sir,' said the claret-liveried porter.

'Splendid day.'

'Lovely, sir, for the time of year.'

'Good morning, Miss Frobisher!'

Aubrey crossed the chessboard floor of the hall.

'Good morning, Mr Whitaker. Beautiful day.'

'Never a better. Morning! Morning!' he greeted Rollo and Bertie, sitting with Herbert in the morning room.

'You're in good form today,' Rollo complained mildly.

Bertie explained: 'Because it's Thursday.'

Aubrey was aghast. 'What? You know about it?'

Bertie was puzzled. 'We all know about it.'

'What!'

'Thursday's tripe and onions day.'

'Ah! Of course. I'm very fond of tripe and onions. Morning, Brindles.'

'Good morning, sir. Pinkers?'

'Champers. In a tinnie.'

'Very good, sir.'

Bertie asked solicitously: 'How's old George getting along?'

'Had a postcard from him this morning,' Aubrey told him cheerfully, picking up *Punch*. 'He's never felt fitter.'

Rollo mentioned, chuckling: 'Noticed you brought his missus to the club the other night.'

'She was very upset about George's heart attack,' Aubrey told him reprovingly. 'Must comfort the poor thing.'

Bertie guffawed. 'Didn't look as if she needed much comforting.'

Rollo grinned. 'You struck us as pretty keen on her, old boy.'

Aubrey was outraged. 'What? Nonsense! Simply a social evening. Bit of a bore, actually.'

Rollo laughed loudly. 'You were looking at her, old man, like Billy Bunter at a fruitcake.'

'George is a well-loved member and a credit to the club,' said Aubrey solemnly, struggling to change the subject.

'Don't think I ever read one of old George's books,' Bertie admitted genially. 'Not as good as they're cracked up to be, I believe.'

Aubrey educated him: 'George is a novelists' novelist.'

'What on earth does that mean?'

'I've no idea. It's just what all the critics say. I suppose they mean that people not paid by the newspapers to read them can't understand them.'

'Well, it's a good job the committee don't think him so distinguished a man of letters that the club needs his portrait. They come frightfully expensive.'

Rollo nodded. 'And after a year or two, nobody has the slightest idea who they're of.'

Bertie stared at a mulligatawny study next to Kipling.

'Who *would* that be, I wonder?'

'Looks like Crippen,' said Rollo.

'A bust of George, perhaps?' Bertie suggested vaguely. 'Like Tennyson.'

'They're not inexpensive, either,' Rollo objected.

'Inscribed tankard?'

'Pricey.'

'When he's back in circulation, the club could stand him a cheapish dinner?'

'Heavens, no!' complained Aubrey, looking up from *Punch*. 'He'd have to make a speech, and we all know old George's stories backwards.'

Brindles appeared with tankard on silver tray.

'Thank you, Brindles. George and I have a lot in common,' Aubrey continued justifying himself. He glanced at George's vacant favourite chair and thought: 'And soon we'll have a lot more!'

'Excuse me, sir. There's a telephone call, sir.'

'Oh, how inconvenient, Brindles.'

Leaving champagne beside Lord Curzon, Aubrey strode back to the hall.

The Albany Club shunned the telephone as an intrusive invention until its member Mr Baldwin became Prime Minister in 1923, when it was felt they might be trying to reach him from Downing Street.

The ebony daffodil was installed in a solidly constructed spacious mahogany and plate-glass box behind the porter's lodge, which Aubrey briskly entered.

'Whitaker,' he said into our more modern 'telecommunications'.

'Darling, a weeny something,' said Vanessa. 'I can't make this afternoon.'

'What! Why?'

'My sister's having one of her things.'

'What things?'

'One of her migraine things. She has to lie alone in a darkened room. I've got to take care of the children.'

Aubrey complained shortly: 'I was particularly looking forward to it.'

'Oh, it was always happening to George. I can't tell you the number of times I left the poor man alone in bed. She's had an awful lot of children. Next Thursday, darling.'

'But that's a whole week!'

'It'll be gone in a flash.'

'George may be back from this horrible health place in Sussex,' Aubrey continued in anguish.

'What of it, darling? George is no more my master than I'm your mistress.'

'Why can't her husband take care of the children?'

'He's got a funeral. Bye, darling.'

She blew a kiss down the line.

'Not bad news?' cried Rollo in alarm, as Aubrey returned.

Aubrey muttered: 'The tripe and onions's off.'

He slumped with his champagne into George's chair, picked the *Spectator* from Herbert's elbow and started reading it unseeingly.

Rollo sniffed. 'The tripe and onions can't be off. I can smell it wafting up the back stairs.'

Aubrey threw the *Spectator* aside.

'I must go and pee.'

Tall and dignified at the porcelain stood the new member Dr Lindisfarne-Jones, who Aubrey had heard was the world's leading specialist on something or other.

'Morning, doctor,' said Aubrey, joining him.

'Morning! You came to see my patient in hospital. Brought him some lovely flowers.'

'He's doing very well. Sending comic postcards.' Aubrey concentrated on the business in hand. 'I suppose a heart attack could happen to anyone?' he speculated, zipping.

'Oh, yes. Absolutely anyone.'

'My sort of age?'

'The commonest.'

They crossed to the marble washbasins with brass taps, pile of crisp handtowels and Imperial Leather soap.

'George said – and I suppose he knew what he was talking about – that heart attacks affected the pyknic type.' Aubrey laughed nervously. 'I'd always associated the word with cheerful things, sunshine and salmon sandwiches and chilled hock.'

'It's got a y–'

'Greek. I know,' Aubrey said impatiently. 'Would you say I was the pyknic type, doctor?' he ventured.

'Oh, undoubtedly.'

Aubrey asked earnestly: 'Tell me, doctor, do many middle-aged men feel impelled by the precariousness of life to do stupid things? In the sexual line, I mean.'

The doctor laughed. 'The Germans have a word for it – *Torschlusspanik*.'

'*Torschlusspanik*.' Aubrey nodded. 'Not dangerous, is it?'

'Frightfully! Lots of men suffer fatal heart attacks during sexual intercourse. Illicit intercourse – routine stuff with the wife doesn't raise the blood pressure much.'

Aubrey was aghast. 'What happens to the lady?'

'Crawls out from underneath, I suppose.'

'Would . . . would you say I was healthy?'

'If you want to find out, come and see me in Harley Street. My receptionist will be pleased to make an appointment.'

He left Aubrey staring fearfully at himself in the brown-speckled gold-framed mirror.

6

It was tripe and onions day again.

'Morning, Brindles!'

Aubrey jauntily entered the empty morning room.

'Just check my lunch reservation's all right, Brindles, there's a good chap. Ladies' dining room.'

'Oh, sir. There was a telephone call, sir.'

Aubrey was horrorstruck.

'What? Who?'

'To telephone your office, sir.'

'Ah! I do wish they wouldn't phone me at the club. Smacks of business.'

He entered the mahogany cabinet.

'Whitaker here,' he announced to his secretary in the City.

'Oh, Mr Whitaker! You wanted to use the flat this afternoon?'

'Need a bit of a lie-down. Not feeling very fit.' His voice weakened.

'Poor Mr Whitaker! Like last Thursday. Unfortunately, Mr Summers from New York has managed to get away a day early, and will be landing at Heathrow at three, and the senior partner says you'll have to find somewhere else to lie down, because Mr Summers is very important, and won't do business until he's got over his jet-lag.'

'What!' Aubrey shouted.

He paused. 'How long's it take, Heathrow to the City?'

'We're sending a car. About an hour, I suppose.'

'An hour!' Aubrey suggested desperately: 'But his plane might not be on time.'

'It is, Mr Whitaker, I've just phoned. They have tail-winds.'

'Tail-winds!' he cried in anguish.

He returned to the morning room, ordered a pinkers and sat scowling at his watch.

Vanessa appeared with admirable punctuality in the ladies' entrance at one o'clock.

'How long has lunch at the club, as well as the uneatable dinner, been unisex?' she enquired brightly, sitting at a pink table.

Aubrey replied hastily: 'The committee decided that, as women existed, we'd better make money out of them.'

He picked up the menu.

'I think, under the circumstances, a quick lunch?'

'Of course not! I think, under the circumstances, a long and lingering one,' she told him romantically. 'Surely nothing improves a meal like a warm bedroom to finish it off?'

Aubrey suggested: 'The tripe and onions is very good.'

She said sharply: 'I will not do what we're going to do with a man who's just eaten tripe and onions.'

'Good morning, sir,' said Rosie.

Aubrey murmured absently: 'Good morning, Rosie.'

'Mmmmmmm!' Vanessa took the menu. 'Roast partridge would be nice.'

'There's a thirty-minute wait on the partridge, madam.'

'What of it?' asked Vanessa lightly. 'We can enjoy your lovely starters. I'll have the chef's assiette of crudities.'

'The same,' ordered Aubrey miserably.

'Very good, sir. Your usual plum duff to follow?'

'No, no! No duff.'

He glared at his watch as Rosie left.

'You *are* jumpy, darling,' Vanessa observed. 'You'd think you'd never done it before with anyone.'

'We've got to keep moving,' he told her grimly.

Her big blue eyes widened.

'Why? You said we could stay in the flat all night, if we wanted.'

He announced: 'We've got to get out of it by four.'

She pointed out: 'Four? But that'll hardly give me time to take my earrings off.'

Aubrey mumbled: 'I must get back to the office.'

'So! You put the Stock Exchange before me?'

'No, no! I don't mean that at all.'

She stared. 'Then what do you mean?'

Aubrey could but shrug. He felt he had lost grip on what everything meant. Brindles approached with the wine list.

'Anything, Brindles. Whatever you've got handy.'

'The club Beaujolais, sir? The committee are trying to get rid of it.'

'Anything, anything.'

Vanessa buttered a roll.

'I suppose Gloria thinks you're having a jolly lunch with your pals?'

Aubrey shrugged again, more hopelessly.

She enquired, crunching roll: 'How is Gloria?'

'All right.'

'What's she like in bed?'

'All right.'

'I do hope that poor dear George enjoyed her,' she speculated kindly.

'I hope so, too.'

'With poor dear George it was like a sneeze, you know. I always felt I ought to say afterwards, "Bless you!"'

'Please! I'm not interested.'

She raised her eyebrows. 'I should have thought, in view of this afternoon, you'd be very interested.'

Aubrey said stiffly: 'I prefer not taking an interest in the sex life of other members of the club.'

He looked at his watch again.

'The service here is terrible.'

When they left the club, members were finishing their port and drifting back to Whitehall, Lincoln's Inn, Fleet Street, the City.

'Why can you never find a taxi when you want one?' complained Aubrey angrily, throwing open the front door of the flat and bundling Vanessa into the bedroom.

'But what a charming little apartment!'

Aubrey whipped off his jacket.

Vanessa picked a china ornament from the dressing-table.

'This could be genuine Sèvres.'

She turned it over.

'It *is* genuine Sèvres.'

Aubrey unzipped her dress.

'Aubrey, really! I utterly refuse to be raped.'

Aubrey frenziedly tapped his watch.

'It's three twenty-five!'

'Oh, very well, darling.'

She slipped off her dress and unhooked her 'bra'.

'We mustn't mess up the bed,' he instructed distractedly.

'I can only do my best, darling.'

She took off her 'pants'.

She reclined on the clematis-patterned duvet.

Aubrey ripped off his clothes and threw himself upon her.

She was amused.

'You *are* the dog after the rabbit.'

He corrected her: 'This is the most wonderful moment of my life.'

Smiling, she flattened the tip of his nose with her finger.

'What would they think at the club now?'

'You know, I couldn't possibly have brought myself to do this, if I was likely to bump into George in the club tonight over a pinkers.'

Unexpectedly he laughed.

'What's so funny, darling?'

'Thinking of that story I was telling George when he nearly died. About the couple in bed, and the Frenchman with the sword–'

He gasped. He grasped his chest. He rolled back on the duvet.

'Darling . . . darling . . .' said Vanessa uncertainly.

'Aubrey!' she shrieked.

'Oh, God!' she cried. 'That's two of them.'

7

In our ladies' 'powder' room, Vanessa was preening herself in the gilt-framed mirror above the frilly dressing-table with the silver hairbrushes and velvet pincushion.

Gloria came in.

'Vanessa!'

'Gloria!'

They embraced.

'How lovely! You're dining at the club?'

'Who could refuse? How's Aubrey?' Vanessa enquired tenderly.

'Making an absolutely wonderful recovery on that health farm.'

'Oh, I'm so glad.' Vanessa sprayed behind her ears. 'I really must apologize for the embarrassing circumstances of his heart attack,' she added quickly.

'But Vanessa, dear! Please don't feel put out in the slightest. The same could have happened to George in Cannes, couldn't it?'

'I suppose so,' Vanessa agreed thoughtfully, replacing fragrant spray in handbag.

'And how is George?'

'Gone for a holiday. In Cannes. He's taken the underwater masseuse from the health farm.'

Gloria sniffed. 'Madame Rochas?'

'Do you like it?' asked Vanessa, pleased.

'Delightful.'

'What do you suppose George and Aubrey thought of the whole business?' she reflected.

'Just part of club life, I suppose. Like sharing hair-brushes.'

Vanessa sighed. 'The Albany Club! It's a quaint place.'

'You know,' decided Gloria, adjusting her corsage. 'I approve of gentlemen's clubs. The members get into the habit of behaving like gentlemen inside them. Quite often, they behave like gentlemen outside again.'

Discovering they were waiting for acquainted ladies in the dining room, Bertie and Rollo had combined their two bottles of champagne at the same pink-clothed table. They rose politely as their guests appeared.

Vanessa had a 'fit of the giggles'.

'Gloria, darling,' she choked. 'We've got the last laugh, haven't we?'

Soon they were laughing uproariously, rolling on their chintz chairs. Bertie and Rollo exchanged nervous glances. Brindles had to cross the room, to see what the matter was. Though I believe in the end it was thought a successful evening all round.

The last time I saw George and Aubrey, they were sitting with a pinkers on the bum-warmer.

'Know the second worst thing that ever happened to the club?' Aubrey complained morosely.

'No, dear boy? What?'

'Letting your wife into the place. You know the worst? Letting in mine. Cheers.'

'Cheers.'